SO-AFH-289 41 15

THE
GUN TRAIL

Center Point
Large Print

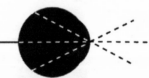

**This Large Print Book carries the
Seal of Approval of N.A.V.H.**

THE
GUN TRAIL

H. A. DeRosso

CENTER POINT LARGE PRINT
THORNDIKE, MAINE

This Center Point Large Print edition is published
in the year 2015 by arrangement with
Golden West Literary Agency.

The text of this Large Print edition is unabridged.
In other aspects, this book may vary
from the original edition.
Printed in the United States of America
on permanent paper.
Set in 16-point Times New Roman type.

ISBN: 978-1-62899-528-2 (hardcover)
ISBN: 978-1-62899-533-6 (paperback)

Library of Congress Cataloging-in-Publication Data

DeRosso, H. A. (Henry Andrew), 1917–1960.
The gun trail / H. A. DeRosso. — Center Point Large Print edition.
pages cm
Summary: "Quinton, a drifter, stands by as a greedy rancher wreaks
havoc throughout the region. No one is safe—not even cattle— as his
gang rides through the hills with a murderous intent. However, when
they point their guns at Quinton, he fights back and the range explodes
into a bloody gun battle"—Provided by publisher.
 ISBN 978-1-62899-528-2 (hardcover : alk. paper)
 ISBN 978-1-62899-533-6 (pbk. : alk. paper)
 1. Large type books. I. Title.
 PS3507.E695G86 2015
 813'.54—dc23
                                                    2015001671

THE
GUN TRAIL

Chapter 1

These mountains were called the White Peaks and, looking at them, he understood why. The highest crests were covered with snow that stayed the whole year round. It made him feel frigid and forlorn just to look at the glaring, aloof whiteness high above him.

He had come a long way, from a town on the Trinity down in Texas. He had crossed the whole long stretch of the state. He had passed into New Mexico and then swung northward. Now he was in Colorado and, for all he knew, no closer to his destination than the day he had left the Trinity. He was beginning to feel that the trail he was riding had no end.

His name was Riley Quinton and he was twenty-eight years old. Sun and wind had darkened the skin of his face. Several days' growth of black beard stubble marked his features.

He was wearing a green flannel shirt, a flannel-lined denim jumper which he had buttoned against the seeping chill of this high altitude, and black woolen trousers thrust into the tops of plain black boots. The gun in the holster at his right hip was a .44 Colt Frontier six-shooter with a seven-and-a-half-inch barrel. The rifle in the saddle scabbard was a Winchester .44-40. He was riding a blaze-faced black that he had acquired in Albuquerque in trade for the hammer-head roan on which he had left the Trinity.

He rode into some trees which were tall enough to cut off the rays of the sun. The black's hoofs made soft sounds crunching on dead pine needles. It was here that Quinton heard the shot.

He emerged from the trees and now the sound came once more, closer. Quinton sent the black up a slope and when he had gained the crest he possessed a good view of the land below him. The ground fell away for quite some distance and far below Quinton could see the floor of a valley. The slopes under him were mottled with clusters of pines and cedars. Between these clusters was open ground and it was in one of these open spaces that Quinton spotted the riders.

There was one horseman in the lead and two in pursuit. They were pounding along the crest of one of the hills that made the foot of the mountain. The first rider had a good lead and appeared to be gaining but this fact did not discourage those in pursuit.

Something caught the corner of Quinton's eye and he looked to his left and there below he saw a lone horseman riding down to the hill along which the other three were racing. This rider's intent was instantly clear to Quinton. This rider meant to intercept the fleeing one.

Quinton threw a swift look at the pursuers and the pursued. Wind whipped the hat off the lead rider's head and Quinton saw the sun blaze in a wealth of bronze hair and it was only then that he knew this was a woman. Those in pursuit of her tried two more shots but they fell short.

Quinton saw that the woman's course was taking her straight toward that other rider who had now dismounted and was waiting, almost directly below Quinton, behind a crag of rock. This fellow was so intent on waiting for the others that he was not aware of Quinton up above. He was not even aware of Quinton when Quinton started the black down the slope.

Quinton skirted a copse of cedar that spotted the side of the hill. This brought him up behind the other who was waiting behind the crag. The man's horse spied Quinton and whinnied. Quinton's black answered. The man came around swiftly, sun glinting off the six-shooter in his hand.

He looked into the bore of Quinton's .44 and the beginning of a snarl died on his face and his mouth slacked a little in fear and consternation. Quinton humped the black up beside the man who was a chunky redhead with red whiskers that blazed like fire in the sun.

Quinton said, "Throw your gun up to me, amigo."

The redhead stood there undecided. Fear and rebellion clashed in the depths of his eyes.

Quinton eared back the hammer of his .44. Beneath him, the black was restless. Quinton had to keep an iron grip on the reins with his left hand. Despite the small jerkings of the black, Quinton's gun never wavered out of line with the redhead's chest.

Quinton said, "I'm not waiting all day. Throw me your gun and do it nice unless you want me to bust a cap." In the distance he could hear the drum of hoofbeats approaching.

"You're taking the wrong side, stranger," said the redhead. He still held his gun.

"I'm not taking any side at all," said Quinton. "I don't like a bushwhack no matter what the circumstances." He wagged his .44. "Toss up your iron, Red."

The redhead bit off a curse. His fingers relaxed about the handle of his .45 and then he worked them so that he held the pistol with the cylinder in his palm. He tossed the gun and Quinton released the reins long enough to catch the weapon with his left hand. He shoved it into his waistband and took up the lines again as the black shied nervously. The drumming hoofbeats were very close now.

"I want to tell you one thing, stranger," said the redhead, his blue eyes clear and unafraid. "Don't stay in the White Peaks. Keep on riding. You've picked the wrong side."

"I stay wherever I please, amigo," said Quinton,

his voice chill. "Save your threats for a woman. That seems to be more your style."

The redhead flushed. He started to say something but then the rider came around the crag and the redhead closed his mouth abruptly.

The woman reined in her palomino so sharply that the horse reared high, front legs pawing the air. He spun half around, carrying the woman away from the crag, but then she saw that Quinton was holding his gun on the redhead and that the redhead was disarmed. With a hard jerk on the lines, she pulled the palomino back, sending it up close to Quinton's black.

Quinton said to the redhead, "Start walking. Tell your friends they're on the wrong trail. Tell them there's nothing here but a slug for each one of them if they don't turn back. Hurry up, amigo."

The woman had pulled a .41 Colt Lightning pistol from the holster at her side. She aimed at the redhead's feet and pulled the trigger. The bullet made the man jump a foot in the air.

"Start walking, Armour," she said, her voice hard. "Do just like the man said. Start walking before I change my mind and put a slug in your heart."

Armour blanched and turned hurriedly on his heel. His spurs made small, protesting noises as he went off at a trot. The instant he was around the crag the nearing hoofbeats slackened and then were still. Quinton heard a horse snort and then his black whinnied.

He edged the black far enough ahead so that he could peer around the crag. Armour was running with his right hand held up in a signal halting the others. They were in the open and when Armour reached them and began to explain, Quinton threw a shot at the ground just in front of them.

They wheeled their horses so suddenly that the animals banged against each other. Armour squalled in fright and threw himself to the ground to avoid colliding with one of the wheeling steeds. Then the riders got straightened out. They headed their horses at a gallop for a clump of trees at the bottom of the hill. Armour jumped to his feet and took out at a run after them, shouting at them, but they did not wait for him.

When Quinton reined the black around, he found the woman's eyes on him. Sunlight set the bronze in her hair aglow. "Thanks, mister," she said. Her voice was low and throaty.

"You're not out of it yet, lady," said Quinton. "How bad do they want you?"

"Bad enough, I guess." Her tone was firm. There was no fear in it.

"Where do you live?"

She waved an arm. "At Anchor. But I have Bar H Bar and Keyhole to cross if I go that way."

Quinton punched the spent shells from his Colt and inserted fresh loads. Then he holstered the gun. He rode the black over to where Armour's horse stood with trailed reins. Quinton picked up the lines.

"Let's get out of here before they circle and come down on us from above."

They rode back up the slope. Quinton was aware of the woman studying him but whenever he glanced at her she was looking down at her horse's ears. When they were at the top of the slope, they reined in. Down below, Quinton saw Armour and the two mounted men emerge from the trees. Sunlight flashed on metal as one of them whipped a rifle to his shoulder.

Quinton and the woman ducked and spurred their horses. The crack of the shot came snaking up the slopes. They sent their horses through a stand of cedar and balsams. The ground began to rise again and they slowed their mounts for the climb. They came out on a high shelf that afforded them a dizzying view of the country below.

They reined in and Quinton dismounted. He stripped bridle and saddle from Armour's horse. Then he clapped the animal on the rump and it went off at a run. Quinton left Armour's saddle on the ground. He swung back up into his kak.

Quinton rolled a smoke. When he was through, the woman said, "Will you roll one for me, too?"

She smiled when Quinton's brows went up. She had small, even teeth that were very white. "Don't you approve of women smoking?"

Quinton said nothing. He handed her the cigarette he had made and then rolled another for himself. He struck a match, lighted her cigarette first, then his own. She took a deep drag on her smoke and then exhaled with a long, audible sigh.

"I sure needed that," she said. She passed the back of a hand over her eyes. At this moment, she looked rather tired.

He said, "My name's Quinton."

"I'm Kate Gillenwater."

She put out her hand and Quinton took it. It felt small and cool in his. Something stirred in him at the contact and he held it tightly a moment. She withdrew it from his fist with a little laugh. Quinton felt his cheeks get warm.

"Can you make it to Anchor all right?" he asked.

She shrugged. "If I don't run into any more of them."

"Why are they after you?"

She smiled. "Maybe they're admirers of mine."

"If I'd known it was a joke," he growled, "I'd have let you be. Maybe you'd like to ride back and join them?"

"I'm sorry," she said, sobering quickly. Sunlight glinted on the highspots of her eyes as she studied him, sweeping him from head to foot. When she spoke, her tone was soft and guarded. "This is a private affair, Quinton. I wouldn't know if you'd care to get involved."

"I'm not looking for trouble," he said.

14

"Then I won't tell you."

Drawing thoughtfully on his smoke, he kneed the blaze-faced black over to the rim of the shelf and carefully scanned the country below. He caught a glimpse of two horses, one of them carrying double, moving down the mountain.

He pinched out his smoke and tossed it over the shelf and watched the butt fall, twirling as it dropped. He lost sight of it before it hit the bottom below. He felt strangely troubled as he reined the black away from the edge of the shell.

He glanced at the woman and saw that she was rubbing out her cigarette on the horn of her saddle. Her head was bowed as she gave all her attention to what she was doing and her profile was framed against the sun. The nose was small with a tilt at the tip. The lips were long and full. A strand of bronze hair had come loose and drifted, almost coquettishly, across the skin of her cheek.

Quinton felt something stirring in him again and the sensation made him a little angry. However, none of this showed in his voice when he said, "Is Gunsight the nearest town?"

She lifted her head and gave him a sharp look. "Is that where you're headed?"

He nodded.

She dropped the dead butt of her smoke to the ground. "Gunsight lies beyond Anchor," she said.

"And Bar H Bar and Keyhole are between us and Anchor?" he asked.

"That's right."

His eyes squinted as he stared at her. "What does that mean?"

She faced him squarely. "Red Armour owns Keyhole."

"The other two," he said. "Are they from Bar H Bar?"

She shook her head. "They're neighbors of Armour's."

"How do we get to Anchor, then?"

"The long way, Quinton," she said. She turned the palomino and then gave Quinton a sidelong look out of her eyes that put a leap in his heart. "We'll have to do a lot of riding. We won't get to Anchor until some time tomorrow . . ."

They stayed just below timberline. The air was thin and cold this high up. Quinton could feel it seeping through his jumper and shirt and woolen trousers. The woman was wearing a bright plaid jacket. It had been open earlier that day but now she buttoned it and then turned the collar up around her neck. She also drew up her hat from where it had been riding on her back, dangling from the chin thongs. She settled the hat on her head and pulled the brim down low over her eyes.

She told Quinton they would have to make a large circle and come in on Anchor from the west. They stayed close to timberline because there were no ranches this high up.

The sun went down and the air grew very cold.

It seemed to whip right off the icy peaks and lay up against Quinton's face with particles of frozen snow in it. The woman was leading the way and now she turned the palomino down the mountainside, seeking a more hospitable altitude before nightfall.

She led the way through a grove of pines that nestled at the edge of a small plateau. They came to a clearing through which a creek ran. The woman dismounted at the edge of the clearing next to the creek. The bank of the pines broke the wind sweeping down from the icy heights. In the last dim light of evening, Quinton gathered some wood and then started the fire.

They had spoken very little the rest of that day and even now they rarely said anything. They went about their tasks almost as if from the force of long habit and Quinton found time to wonder about this. When he thought about it, that strange stirring moved again in him.

The woman cooked a meal out of the supplies Quinton was packing with him. He staked out the horses and then he sat on his saddle where it lay on the ground and smoked a cigarette and watched her. Her hair looked a bright red where it reflected the light of the fire. Even the skin of her face had a reddish tint against the firelight. Quinton was watching her like this when he spotted the wedding band on her finger.

He could not understand why it should have

startled him. For several moments he knew the galling taste of disappointment. Then he began to think that it was better this way.

When they had eaten and the tin plates and cups had been washed, she asked Quinton to roll her another cigarette. Quinton had split his bedroll, placing half the blankets on one side of the fire for her and the other half on the opposite side for himself. She was wearing gray woolen trousers and, after removing her boots, she tucked her legs under a blanket and then sat there like that while she smoked. When she was done, she tossed the butt into the fire.

She drew up her knees and clasped her arms about them and for a while she sat like that, huddled over, one cheek resting on her knees. Quinton got up and put more wood on the fire. Then he stood looking down at the woman. He felt very grave and almost sad inside. She became aware of his study and she turned her eyes enough to catch sight of him and then she stayed like that, eyes regarding him soberly out of their corners, her cheek still resting on her knees.

He thought of the last time he had had a woman and then, angrily, he put the recollection from him. It was no good thinking about a thing like that. Tomorrow they would part and he would never see her again, and, looking at the wedding band that was reflecting the light of the fire at this moment, he was glad. He turned and went back to his blankets.

He had placed his saddle at the head of his blankets since he used the kak for a pillow. He sat down on the saddle and took out the makin's and when he had them in his hand he wondered why he was holding them since he did not feel like another smoke.

The woman said, "Where are you from, Quinton?"

Glancing at her, he saw that she had straightened up. She still sat with her legs under a blanket. With her hands she fluffed out the ends of her bronze hair that reached down to her shoulders.

"South a ways," he said.

"You sound like Texas."

"That's right."

"What part of Texas?"

Caution made him think a moment, eyes crinkling. Then he said, "From around El Paso. You ever been there, ma'am?"

"No." She was done with her hair. She picked up a stick and, leaning over, poked at the fire. Pitch sizzled and a few sparks leaped up. "Do you aim to stop long in Gunsight?"

"That all depends," he said, suddenly thinking of the job that had brought him here from the Trinity.

She let the fire alone and he could feel her glance across the top of the flames. It was level

19

and searching and even bold, but he put that down to a trick of the firelight.

"Drifting, Quinton?" she asked.

He nodded.

"I'd say it's a pretty lonely life."

"It is," he said.

"Why don't you get yourself a wife, Quinton?"

He did not answer. His throat was dry and aching.

"You're a good man, Quinton," she said. "Find yourself a wife and settle down. You'll find it's the best life in the world."

He said nothing. He watched as she got down between the blankets. She rolled herself tightly in them with her back to the fire. Her voice came, faint and muffled.

"Goodnight, Quinton."

"Goodnight."

A pine knot exploded with a sound as loud and sharp as a gunshot. The smoke from the fire rose in twining, writhing twirls. Quinton sat and watched the fire a long time.

Quinton was up at dawn. He built up the fire and then he took the coffee pot down to the creek and came back with some water. He poured in the coffee and set the pot on the fire. He tried to be quiet but still he made some noise and it woke the woman.

She sat up and then gently scolded him for not having waked her earlier. There was a smile in her voice and in her eyes and Quinton answered her with a smile of the lips. He said nothing. He felt he didn't need any words right now.

She pulled on her boots and then she took over the preparation of breakfast while Quinton cared for the horses. After they had eaten, Quinton saddled the animals while she washed the cups and pans and put them away. They rode off with the sun shining on the high peaks but with shadow still in the valleys.

By the middle of the morning they had completed their circle and began coming in from the west. The woman appeared elated and Quinton surmised they were out of danger. He was sure of it when he spotted some white-faces carrying the Anchor brand.

They came to a road and the woman reined in her palomino. She waved a hand. "Gunsight is that way, Quinton. Follow this road and you can't miss it."

He touched his hat and started to rein the black away when she said, "Will I ever see you again, Quinton?"

No, he told himself as he turned to look at her once more. But to her he said, "I couldn't say, ma'am."

Her face looked grave and wistful. She lifted a hand to fluff out her hair and the sun flashed off the wide wedding band. It threw the reflected light almost mockingly in Quinton's eyes.

"You'll always be welcome at Anchor, Quinton," she said. "Remember that."

"I will," he said, trying to keep the sadness out of his voice.

He touched the brim of his hat once more and then brushed the black lightly with the spurs. The horse started down the road toward Gunsight.

Chapter 2

Quinton reached Gunsight late that afternoon. He put the black up at a livery and then he registered for a room at the Continental Hotel. After that, he took a turn down the wind-swept street of Gunsight until he found a barber shop. He had the whiskers taken off his face and then he had a hot bath and when he stepped out on the street again he felt like a new man.

The sun had gone down behind a snow-capped peak and shadow lay over Gunsight which was situated at the base of the mountain. Quinton had dinner in the Continental's dining room and then he went upstairs.

In his room, he lit the lamp and sat down on the edge of the bed and pulled off his boots. Unbuckling his shell belt, he hung it from the bedstead. Then he built a smoke and stretched out on the bed with a sigh of comfort and relief.

He lay there, drawing slowly and with relish on his cigarette, blowing the smoke up and watching how it eddied there. After a while, he began to see a face in the haze. It was a beautiful face framed in a mass of flaming bronze hair. He cursed and sat up on the edge of the bed again.

He took a paper out of his pocket and unfolded

it and studied the picture and description as he had studied them so many times before. He felt he did not need the reward poster any more. He was positive he would recognize the man the instant he laid eyes on him even though he had never seen the fellow in the flesh. Quinton had carried that picture and description in his mind all the way from the Trinity.

After a while, Quinton refolded the poster and put it away. The paper was beginning to be badly worn at the creases from having been handled so much. He undressed, blew out the light and got in bed.

He slept well into daylight. The sun's rays were slanting through the window directly on his face when he batted his eyes open. He threw off the covers and rose to his feet.

He washed up out of the porcelain basin on the chest of drawers. Then he dressed. He belted on his gun and then checked the loads out of an old caution. He felt refreshed and even a little jaunty this morning and his spurs seemed to jingle a happy melody as he went out.

The wind had died during the night. Wood-smoke thrust straight up out of the chimneys of the town. The dust lay dormant and listless on the rutted main drag.

Quinton remembered a cafe next to the barber shop and he went there for breakfast. He didn't know whether it was town cooking or the altitude that gave him such an appetite. He had a large steak and potatoes, three cups of coffee and two slabs of apple pie. The world looked bright and pleasant to him when he walked out of the cafe.

He paused on the walk to let his belt out a notch and it was then that Quinton saw the riders. There were three of them coming down the main drag, their horses moving at a walk. Two of them Quinton had never seen. Recognition of the third rider hit Quinton like a kick between the eyes.

This was the first time Quinton had seen the man in the flesh but it was like seeing someone he had known all his life. On the instant, he could not believe that the long search was over. He had become so reconciled to the interminability of it that at first his mind could not register the fact that the trail from the Trinity had come to an end here in Gunsight.

As he rode past, the man turned his head and laid a look on Quinton but it was an impersonal, disinterested stare. Quinton's heart hit a hammerstroke, then quieted. There was no way for the fellow to know who Quinton was. Quinton hadn't come to the town on the Trinity until the man had killed and fled.

The riders passed on. Quinton stood there, watching them go. His heart picked up again, he could hear its beat in his ears. The three pulled up their horses in front of the Silver Spur, which was a bar, and dismounted. One of them crossed the street and went into the general store. The man from the Trinity and his companion entered the Silver Spur.

There was a tightness in Quinton's throat as he started for the saloon. He loosened the .44 in its holster without being aware of doing so. The toes of his boots kicked up small puffs of dust that quickly settled in the windless air.

His lips were thin and dry when he pushed through the swing doors of the Silver Spur and stepped inside. He paused while his eyes picked out the two, standing close together in the middle of the bar. They were the only drinkers in the place.

At the sound of the doors opening, the man from the Trinity turned his head. He had pale eyes that were as expressionless as the unseen bottom of a deep well. He had unbuttoned his mackinaw and had brushed the bottom of it back. Twin belts were strapped about his waist. Each belt supported a .44 Remington in a tied-down holster.

Now something seeped into Quinton's awareness. It was something that had existed ever since he had arrived in Gunsight, but he had been caught up too much in his own problems to have given it any thought. It was a feeling of tension, of a great and portentous something hanging uneasily over the town. He remembered Kate Gillenwater and Red Armour and the other two, and now Quinton wondered if the man from the Trinity was a part of it, too.

Quinton took two more steps ahead and then he stopped. The man from the Trinity seemed to become aware that this was meant for him. His whole body turned now so that he faced Quinton squarely. A spur sounded softly as the fellow moved enough away from the bar so that his arms swung free. The import of what was building up struck his companion at this time and he also turned around to face Quinton.

Quinton's throat was so dry it ached when he swallowed. He could not help thinking that down on the Trinity this fellow had killed three men in a running gunfight. That was an eloquent evaluation of his deadliness.

Quinton was about to speak when he heard the swing doors creak behind him. Turning his head that way, he saw the third man, the one who had gone into the store across the way. The fellow pulled up just across the threshold, wind-burned face instantly alert as he took in the setup before him.

He paused like that, dark eyes studying Quinton. After a moment, the man's glance swung to the two at the bar. "I'm all through, Stony," the man said.

The fellow from the Trinity grunted. Those pale eyes hung on to Quinton's an instant longer. Then it became apparent to the man that Quinton was not going to do anything. With a jerk of his head the fellow summoned his companion. Together they walked to the door and passed through. The third man went out after them.

The palms of Quinton's hands were sweating.

From outside came the creak of saddle leather as the three mounted. When the horses moved away, Quinton went up to the doors and pushed through. He paused just outside and watched the three riding down the main drag. They passed the livery and all three waved to someone in a corral. Then they turned down a side street and were gone from sight.

Quinton walked to the stable. In the corral, an old-timer was forking hay for some horses. Quinton put a boot on the lowest pole of the corral fence and said:

"Who were those three riders who just went by, Pop?"

The old-timer looked up with a crinkling of the eyes. The wrinkles were very deep and very dark as if they had been worked upon by the sun and wind of countless years.

"Which riders?" said the old man.

"The three who just went by. One rode a roan, one a paint and one a buckskin. Who are they?"

The old-timer stuck the tines of his fork in the ground and leaned on the handle. He was working on a chew and tobacco juice drooled out of the corner of his mouth and soiled his white whiskers.

"Why you asking?" he said.

"They looked like cattlemen to me," said

Quinton, "and I'm looking for a riding job."

The old man considered this. His eyes swept Quinton with a live interest. They looked shrewd and calculating when they stared at the hang of Quinton's gun.

"What kind of wages you expecting?" the old man asked.

"What kind of wages do they pay around here?"

"Just about every kind. Depends what you hire out for," said the old-timer, giving another look at Quinton's .44.

"Is something going on around here?" asked Quinton.

The man spat and then stared at the brown stain a while as if reading sign in the pattern. Then he came over and leaned against the corral fence next to Quinton. The old man's eyes were cold.

"If you want to hire out your gun," he said, his voice as hard as his eyes, "go see Clay Gillenwater at Anchor. He'll pay you all of two hundred a month."

"And if I don't want to hire my gun?" asked Quinton.

The old-timer's glance dropped to the .44 at Quinton's side. The whiskered jaws moved steadily but the old-timer did not speak.

"What's stopping you, Pop?" Quinton asked.

The old man's glance rose and locked with Quinton's in a challenge. "I've been around, son," the old man said. "You don't wear that iron because it makes you look purty."

"Neither does one of those riders who just passed by," said Quinton softly, "and he wears two irons."

"He wears them in a good cause," said the old man with some heat.

"Oh?" said Quinton. "Maybe I'd like to wear mine the same way."

"I wish you would," said the old man. "They sure could use another man like Stony Brice."

Down on the Trinity he had been Steve Bryan, Quinton thought. Here in the White Peaks they called him Stony Brice. "Who does Brice work for?" Quinton asked.

"Aren't you interested in Anchor?" the old man parried.

"What's going on around here, Pop? I'm a stranger and I'd appreciate you setting me straight before I get mixed up with the wrong side."

"I'm not saying there's any wrong side." The man spoke with the semblance of a growl. "I'm a nobody myself and maybe that's why I feel the way I do. I used to be a cowpuncher once but now I'm old and I couldn't even rope a tumbleweed. All I'm good for is to swamp around a stable," he said with a touch of bitterness. "It isn't that I'm against them that have but I feel they should be satisfied with what they've got and not try to grab more."

"Is that what Anchor's trying to do?"

The old man nodded and swore. "Anchor's the biggest spread in these parts. Anchor's got more graze and more cows than Clay Gillenwater knows what to do with but that don't satisfy him. He wants everything this side of the White Peaks and if he ever gets it, I don't think he'll be satisfied even then."

"What about Brice?" asked Quinton.

"He came here about a month ago and surprised everybody by going to work for Wes Hawthorne. Wes runs Bar H Bar and he organized the boys to stand up to Anchor but they weren't getting anywhere until Brice came. Fellows like Hawthorne are ranchers, they're not fighters. That's where Brice comes in. He knows how to stand up to Anchor and its hired gunslingers. Without Brice, I don't know what Hawthorne and the others would do . . ."

Quinton sighted the buildings of Bar H Bar early in the afternoon. A dog barked as he rode into the yard. He reined in the black and glanced about him. The buildings of Bar H Bar were set in the hollow between two ranges of hills. The house was small but sturdy, the kind of structure a man who lives alone might build. The hip-roofed barn and the sheds and corrals were in excellent repair.

The dog barked again and came bounding out

from around a corner of the house. He circled the black, giving throat to his alarms all the while, and the black began to shy nervously. Quinton maintained a firm pressure on the reins and spoke soothingly to the horse.

The door of the house opened. A man stepped out and said something sharply to the dog. The dog quit his yapping and slunk off. The man came ahead a couple of steps and stopped. Quinton sent the black up to the fellow. It was the same man who had come into the Silver Spur so inopportunely for Quinton that morning.

The man, however, gave no indication that he recognized Quinton. "Light and rest your saddle, stranger," the man said. He was bare-headed and the breeze ruffled his thick, iron-gray curls. His dark eyes looked veiled and cautious.

A faint uneasiness stirred in Quinton. He gave a look around but saw nothing out of the ordinary. He dismounted and stretched to get the saddle stiffness out of his bones.

"Are you Wes Hawthorne?" Quinton asked.

The man nodded. The breeze plucked at the sleeves of his red and black woolen shirt, molding them against his large biceps. A .45 Colt was in the holster at his right hip.

Quinton was about to speak when, glancing up at the house, he saw that the door was half open. He also saw the bore of a rifle pointing at him.

Hawthorne smiled slightly when he saw the

look of dismay on Quinton's face. However, the smile vanished quickly. Hawthorne drew his .45. Without a word, he stepped around behind Quinton and took Quinton's gun.

Then Hawthorne said, "Let's go into the house, friend."

Quinton could hear the sledging of his heart as he walked up to the door. The bore of the rifle never left him. He paused at the step and Hawthorne poked him in the back with the .45. Quinton stepped into the house.

This was the kitchen. A stove was against one wall and opposite it was a table surrounded by four chairs. In one of the chairs sat Stony Brice but it was not sight of him that startled Quinton. It was the man holding the rifle.

He had drawn to one side as Quinton entered. There was a big, gloating smile on the fellow's red-bearded face. He said, "You didn't leave the White Peaks, did you, mister? That was a big mistake for you."

Quinton said nothing. Wes Hawthorne motioned with his .45 at one of the chairs.

"Have a seat, friend."

Quinton sat down at the table across from Brice. The man from the Trinity was studying his nails. He had not looked once at Quinton.

When Brice would not glance at him, Quinton shifted his gaze to Hawthorne. "What is this, Hawthorne?" he asked.

"I could ask you the same thing," said Hawthorne.

"I rode in peaceable, didn't I?"

"Yes, you did," said Red Armour with the touch of a snarl. "But I happened to be here. That was something you weren't expecting. You figured Wes wouldn't know about you and Kate Gillenwater." His mouth contorted in an angry grimace. "You should have ridden on like I told you two days ago. You'd have played it smart then."

"What there is between you and Mrs. Gillenwater," said Quinton, "is none of my business. I've no intention of making it my business either. I just don't like the idea of three men ganging up on a woman. I told you that, Red."

"Ya-aah," Armour said jeeringly. "We've got something besides rocks in our heads."

"What's your name?"

It was Brice who asked this. He spoke quietly, even deferentially, in a voice soft as a woman's. He sat there with his head bowed a little. He had taken out a pocket knife and with this he was paring his nails. Quinton saw the wind-burned curve of his cheek and the rather handsome, boyish profile and he found himself wondering if this was really the man who had killed three hardcases back on the Trinity.

"Quinton. Riley Quinton."

"Are you from Texas?"

"That's right."

Brice straightened out the fingers of his left hand and critically studied the job he was doing on his nails. His fingers were long and slim, almost feminine. "What part of Texas?" he asked in that soft, polite tone.

Quinton hesitated the barest moment. "From around El Paso," he said.

"You ever been anywhere else?"

"I've been south of El Paso, in Mexico."

"I mean anywhere else in Texas?"

"I passed through the Panhandle three years back."

The knife made soft, scraping sounds as Brice used it again. "What are you doing in the White Peaks?"

"Drifting."

"Drifting where?"

Quinton shrugged. He kept staring at Brice's profile but Brice continued to give all his attention to scraping his nails.

"Drifting where, Quinton?" Brice asked again. There was just a barely perceptible hardening of his tone.

"I couldn't say. I just keep heading for the other side of the horizon."

"What did you want with me in the Silver Spur?"

"I don't know what you mean."

"You acted like you knew me."

"I made a mistake," said Quinton. He hoped

35

he sounded calm and convincing. "I've drifted around pretty much and at first I thought you were somebody I knew. Then I took another look and saw that you weren't."

Brice shut his knife with a loud snap. Then he turned his head and glanced at Quinton. Those pale eyes mirrored as much emotion as the icy crests of the White Peaks. Nevertheless, they studied Quinton very carefully, probing at his face, searching it for some hidden meaning, appraising the shape of his shoulders and the slant of the shell belt at his waist and the hang of the empty holster.

Brice stretched a hand out toward Hawthorne. "Let me see his iron, Wes."

Hawthorne passed the .44 to Brice. He took his glance off Quinton and regarded the Colt with a thoughtful preoccupation. Brice tested the spring on the hammer by working it back and forth several times. He spun the cylinder and watched it whirl easily on its well-oiled shaft. Then he hefted the gun a while.

"When you're not drifting, Quinton," he said, still staring at the .44, "what do you work at?"

Quinton shrugged. His manner was nonchalant. "Anything I can get. Mostly punching cows."

"Why did you come to Bar H Bar?"

"I thought Hawthorne might be hiring."

"Spy!" Armour burst out with a display of vehemence. His fists clenched and his body inclined forward at the waist from the fury that raged in him. "That's what he aimed to be. A dirty, stinking spy. Kate Gillenwater put him up to it. Hire out to Bar H Bar and then spy for Anchor!"

"Take it easy, Red," said Wes Hawthorne.

Quinton said, "Would Anchor send me here after what I did two days ago and after the good look Red got of me? If Anchor ever sends a spy, it will be someone none of you have ever seen before."

"Are you denying you work for Anchor?" asked Brice.

"I've never been on Anchor."

"That don't mean a thing," cried Armour, eyes glaring. "Kate Gillenwater could have hired you on the sly. We know all about you Texas gunmen, Quinton. Anchor's brought in several of you."

"Is that how you got Brice?" asked Quinton.

In the silence, they could hear the wind rattling something against the house. Red Armour was breathing with heavy, stentorian sounds. Wes Hawthorne laid a quick, anxious look on Stony Brice.

"Is there any other reason why I should have left Texas?" he asked in a tone as soft and non-committal as if he were asking about the weather.

"People leave Texas for many reasons," Quinton said. If he knows who I am he'll kill me, he thought. With my own gun he'll kill me. "I wouldn't know what yours was."

Brice flipped the loading gate of the .44 open

and studied the brass head of a shell. "Why did you leave Texas, Quinton?"

"I told you. I'm drifting."

Brice looked at Hawthorne. "What do you think, Wes?" Brice asked.

Hawthorne's eyes narrowed a little as he thought. He was a big-chested man of around fifty, slow and methodical and innately cautious. "I wouldn't trust him," he said after a while. "He might be speaking the truth because I don't think Anchor would send him to spy after he had that run-in with Red and the boys. Still I won't trust him. I won't trust anybody who's had anything to do with Anchor."

"I still say Anchor sent him," cried Red Armour, his mind still on the same track. "Why else would he come? He's a gunman and Anchor's the only outfit hiring gunmen. I say string him up and then send his corpse back to Anchor. That'll teach them to send us spies!"

Brice studied the .44 a while longer. Then he tipped up the barrel and, one by one, dropped out the cartridges. He shoved the empty gun across the table at Quinton.

"The only reason we're letting you go, Quinton," he said quietly, his eyes as cold as death, "is that you might be telling the truth. If you are, then drift on and that will be the end of it. But if you hang around the White Peaks, let me tell you this. You and me will meet again, amigo."

Chapter 3

In the morning he had to curb his eagerness. He forced himself to eat a leisurely breakfast and then he strolled to the stable. The old man looked inquiringly at Quinton but Quinton mounted and rode away without a word.

The Trinity seemed a long way back in his memory and he found himself wondering if he would ever see it again. He did not miss it because it was not his country. He had been born in the Big Bend part of Texas. However, he had been around. He thought of himself as an itinerant lawman. He worked as a deputy wherever the job was available. He was a good man hunter, and word of this had got to the sheriff on the Trinity and he had sent for Quinton. Now Quinton was here in the White Peaks, and so was the man he was after.

He followed the road and at Anchor's gate he turned off. Almost instantly he had the feeling that he was under surveillance but when he looked about he saw no one.

He passed scattered bunches of white-faces. All of them wore the Anchor brand and they looked sleek and fat. He rode to the top of a hill and because the feeling was still on him he reined in the black and made a careful study of all the land. But he saw no one.

He saw a rider only once. The horseman silhouetted himself briefly on a hilltop and then was gone. Probably heading for the ranch buildings to report his approach, Quinton thought. Those hidden eyes stayed on his back.

He topped another rise and there ahead lay the buildings of Anchor. They had been erected in the center of a long stretch of level ground. The hills thrust up in the distance all about them and beyond the hills was the massive, white-capped rise of the mountains. Clumps of trees broke the monotony of green graze.

The buildings of Anchor were large and numerous. The house was a huge, rambling structure, built of stone save for the roof and eaves. A gallery ran the whole long length of the place and Quinton saw two men standing there as he rode up.

There was nothing of friendliness or welcome in the air of Anchor. Tension and hostility were almost palpable things. Again Quinton had the impression of eyes covertly watching him. It set tiny, chill fingers to feeling his spine.

One of the men on the gallery stirred and then stepped down to the ground and walked out to meet Quinton. He reined in the black and looked down. The fellow had no detectable expression on his face as he stared up at Quinton.

"Who's the ramrod here?" Quinton asked.

The fellow's eyes were a dark shade of green. Squint wrinkles edged the corners and gave him the look of being constantly engrossed in profound thought. "What you want with the ramrod?" the fellow said. His voice darned the twang of Texas.

"I'm looking for a job."

The fellow thought on this a while. He dropped his glance from Quinton's face down to Quinton's gun and, after a while, raised it again. "We're full up," he said.

"How do you know?" asked Quinton.

"I'm the ramrod."

Quinton shifted his gaze to the other man who was still standing on the gallery. He was a big fellow and he was smoking a cigar and watching Quinton steadily. Quinton turned his look back to the ramrod.

"I was told by Mrs. Gillenwater," Quinton said, "that a job would be here for me if I ever wanted it. My name's Quinton."

A look of sharp interest entered the ramrod's eyes. He lifted a hand and pulled at the tip of his prominent nose. Then he turned his head and threw a glance at the man on the gallery.

"Who did he say he was, Dalhart?" this man asked the ramrod.

Dalhart said simply, "Quinton."

The man on the gallery beckoned Quinton with a jerk of the head. The fellow did it brusquely and even a little imperiously as if he were long accustomed to directing men with the briefest of signals and being instantly obeyed. Quinton sent the black ahead, trying hard not to let this arrogance get him.

The man took a deep drag on his cigar and then exhaled the smoke. It lingered in front of his face in the still air of the gallery and the men studied Quinton through the blue haze. "I'm Clay Gillenwater," the big man said. "I want to thank you for helping Mrs. Gillenwater the other day."

Quinton acknowledged the thanks with a nod of his head. He did not speak. He waited for Gillenwater to continue.

Gillenwater took the cigar out of his mouth and flicked ash off the end. He was a man in his middle thirties. His waist showed the beginnings of a paunch but there was nothing soft about it or him. He had hair as dark as Quinton's and a black mustache drooped down around the corners of Gillenwater's mouth. His fresh-shaved jowls were blue.

"Why do you want to go to work for Anchor?" he asked.

Quinton shrugged. "I'm broke."

"You a drifter?" Gillenwater asked. His coal-black eyes strayed briefly to Quinton's .44.

"I move around," Quinton said, "but I can stay put a while if I have to."

"Do you know anything of the trouble between

Anchor and the other outfits of the White Peaks?"

"I've heard some talk," Quinton said guardedly.

"How was that talk?" asked Gillenwater.

Quinton glanced at Dalhart and caught the ramrod staring at him with a studied concentration. Dalhart looked away hurriedly, then his eyes came back and stayed on Quinton, defiantly. Quinton shifted his attention back to Clay Gillenwater.

"I don't hold much with gossip," Quinton said slowly. "I believe only what I see for myself."

Gillenwater sucked on his cigar, seeming deep in thought. After a while, he said, "I expect the utmost of loyalty from all my men. I expect all my orders to be obeyed and executed instantly and without questioning. I will not tolerate idling or malingering. I will not stand for any fraternizing with the hands of the other spreads in the White Peaks. If these conditions suit you, Quinton, Dalhart will show you where to bunk."

Quinton got his roll from behind his saddle and carried it in the bunkhouse. Dalhart was there and he indicated a wooden bunk with a nod of his head. Quinton dumped his roll there. He could feel Dalhart's eyes studying him keenly.

"What part of Texas are you from, Quinton?" asked Dalhart.

"El Paso." He was getting used to saying it, he thought. It came to him automatically and unhesitatingly as if it were the truth.

43

"You're a long way from home," said Dalhart.

"No farther than you."

Dalhart bowed his head as if thinking on something. Quinton had a look of the ramrod's profile. The prominent, hooked nose gave a cruel and predatory cast to Dalhart's features. After a moment, Dalhart's head lifted and he laid another calculative glance on Quinton's .44.

"Are you any good with that iron?" he asked softly.

"I know which end the bullet comes out of," Quinton said dryly.

The slight hint of a flush touched the highspots of Dalhart's cheeks. His lips thinned. "You better get this straight right at the beginning, Quinton," he said darkly. "I'm ramrod here and what I say goes. If there's one thing I don't like it's an hombre with smart-aleck answers. Remember that and me and you will get along all right."

With that, Dalhart turned so sharply that his spurs shrilled. He stalked out of the bunkhouse. Quinton watched him go with a slight, mirthless smile on his lips.

He went out, unsaddled his black and turned the horse into a corral that held several other ponies. He carried his kak to the saddle shed and when he came out a rider on a well-groomed buckskin passed Quinton by.

The fellow reined in when he spied Quinton. He pulled the buckskin around and then the fellow leaned forward a little in his kak and folded his hands over the horn. He had snow-white hair and the skin of his face held the many deep creases of old age but his shoulders were still erect and his light blue eyes were bright and young.

"You're another one," he said, more to himself than to Quinton.

"Another what?" asked Quinton.

"Another gunman from Texas."

A fit of irritation passed through Quinton. He eyed the handle of the .44 Starr jutting out of the old fellow's holster. "I'm not the only one hereabouts packing a gun," he said.

"It's not the packing of a gun that's bad," said the old man, his eyes hardening. "It's the way it's used."

"What makes you think I'll be using mine?"

"You've hired out to Anchor, haven't you?"

Quinton paused and took another, more deliberate look of the old fellow. Under a close-cropped mustache the man's lips were pinched, mirroring a mixture of sadness and helpless anger. His large hands closed tightly about the horn and squeezed until the knuckles showed palely through the straining skin.

"Are you with Anchor?" Quinton asked softly.

"I helped build Anchor," said the old fellow, a bit of wistfulness in his voice. "I came to the White Peaks from Texas with Colonel Gillenwater almost forty years ago. I ramrodded Anchor until

45

I decided to get a place of my own. My brand is Broken Bit and my name is Luke Fowler."

"I'm Quinton."

"Why don't you go back to Texas, Quinton?"

"Is there a reason why I should?"

"There will be dying before this is over," said Fowler, his eyes veiled and sad. The corner of his mouth twitched once in a spasm of futile rage. "Do you want blood on your hands, Quinton?"

"What makes you think I'm a gunman?"

"Anchor wouldn't have hired you if you weren't."

"Don't you think it's my business and mine alone who I hire out to?" he asked, a growl in his tone.

"Is he giving you a bad time, Quinton?"

At the words, Quinton turned his head and saw Clay Gillenwater coming up. There was a strange grimace on Gillenwater's lips that could have been either wry humor or real displeasure.

"Are you preaching to my men again, Luke?" asked Gillenwater. His tone was mild but his dark eyes were hard.

Fowler reined his buckskin a little so that he faced Gillenwater squarely. Angry color touched the crests of Fowler's cheeks. "Don't you have enough gunslingers an Anchor, Clay? How many more are you going to bring in?"

"Anchor's growing," Gillenwater said blandly. "I need more punchers all the time. That's what

I'm hiring. Cowpunchers. You're getting worked up about nothing, Luke."

"I saw it coming when you hired Dalhart," Fowler said, eyes bright with righteous rage. His fingers kept opening and closing about the horn. "I warned you then but you kept right on and you brought in Slim Sunderland and Frio Bates and George Marberry and now Quinton. Do you call that nothing, Clay?"

Gillenwater's chest swelled as he inhaled deeply. Anger bunched the muscles along his jaw but then he bowed his head and studied the ground as he fought to contain his wrath. When he raised his hand, his face was pale.

"What have you got to gripe about?" said Gillenwater. "I'm not after Broken Bit."

"That's not enough for me," said Fowler. The buckskin stirred restlessly and Fowler reined it in with a hard hand. "You can't buy me off that way."

"I'm not buying you off. I'm doing it for old times' sake."

"You don't owe me anything for old times, Clay. I always told the Colonel he spoiled you. He should have taken the quirt to you a few times."

Gillenwater's chest swelled again. "You can't talk to me like that, Luke."

"I'll talk to you any way I please. You might have everybody else in this country buffaloed, but not me. Isn't Anchor big enough for you? Why do you want Bar H Bar and all the other spreads? What's got into you, Clay?" There was a plaintive note to Fowler's last words.

"Those greasy sack outfits are a bunch of thieves," said Gillenwater with vehemence. "I've had my fill of them running off my cattle and cutting my fences. There's room for only one outfit in the White Peaks—and that's Anchor."

"What about Broken Bit?"

"That's for you to decide, Luke. I'm only telling you not to take sides."

"That's going to be pretty hard to do if you don't stop bringing in these Texas gunmen."

"Is that a threat, Luke?"

Fowler straightened in the saddle and picked up the lines. He wrapped the ends tightly about one hand and pulled until the skin turned white. Sadness dulled the luster of his eyes.

"There are times when I tell myself I could hate you, Clay," Fowler said quietly, "but then I remember all the times I rocked you on my knee. I braided your first rope for you. I taught you how to use it until you were the best man with a rope in the White Peaks. We had a lot of good times in the past, Clay. I've never married. You're the only family I ever had. I keep remembering that when everything in me tells me to hate you because you've grown mean and hateful."

Gillenwater raised a hand and brushed it lightly against his mustache. The agate hardness of his eyes mirrored nothing. "I keep remembering, too, Luke. That's why I won't touch Broken Bit. I'll take a lot from you but don't stretch your luck. Remember that."

Quinton did not see the bronze-haired woman until the next day. He dreamed of her that night, a strange, troubled dream that left him rather forlorn and disappointed when he awoke. He did not like this but there was nothing he could do about it.

He and another hand, a young fellow named Bucky Dean, were repairing the chuck wagon. Dalhart had appeared to experience a mean pleasure when he had assigned this job to Quinton. Quinton, however, had shrugged off any resentment. A natural dislike already lay between him and Dalhart and he had no desire to antagonize the foreman any further.

Quinton and Dean were greasing the axles when Kate Gillenwater came out of the big house and headed for the corrals. Quinton happened to glance up and when he saw her, he froze as he was, for the instant mesmerized by the sight of her. She had her hat hanging by the chin thongs down her back, and sunlight rioted in her hair. Her plaid jacket was open at the front, revealing the scarlet shirt underneath and beneath this was apparent the prominent roundness of her breasts.

She passed Quinton by without a glance at him and he was sure she had not noticed him.

Disappointment lay like a knife-edge against his heart. But as she pulled away, she said:

"Saddle my horse, Quinton."

He felt his heart give a leap. "The palomino?" he asked.

"Of course."

He got his rope and went into the corral and snared the palomino. He slipped on the bridle and cinched on the kak and led the animal over to the woman who was standing there, staring at nothing.

He held the bridle while she swung up into the saddle with a lithe, graceful movement. He handed her the lines and she took them, flicking his face with a glance that was brief and impersonal. Then she touched the horse with silvered spurs and rode off.

Quinton turned to watch her go. In his heart there was a feeling of frustration and bafflement. He told himself he should not have expected anything, considering that she was another man's wife. It was best this way. He could not have hoped for anything else. Still, disappointment and hurt lay heavy on his heart.

He watched until she rode over a rise out of sight. Then he turned back to the wagon and found young Bucky Dean studying him. The youth's eyes reflected a wisdom and understanding far beyond his years.

"She's a mighty purty woman," Dean murmured.

Quinton felt his face grow a trifle warm. Angrily, he grabbed a wheel and slid it on the axle. "How long have they been married?" he asked. In his ears, his voice sounded gruff.

"About two years. The boss married her right after the Colonel died."

"Is she from around here?"

"She's never said where's she's from. She drifted into Gunsight about two and a half years ago and began dealing faro in the Palace. Every man in the White Peaks made a play for her. I was kind of stuck on her myself," said the youth with a small, self-conscious laugh. "But I was only eighteen years old and then Clay Gillenwater started courting her in earnest. She didn't surprise any one when she married him."

"Is she always this snooty?"

Dean did not answer right away. He raised a freckled hand and rubbed his chin thoughtfully. His eyes grew a little veiled. "She's married to the owner of the biggest ranch in these parts. Me and you—we're just hired hands." He paused and then went on, awkwardly, "It's all right to look, now and then, Quinton. But that's about all. Do you get what I mean?"

The next day Quinton and Dean were detailed to check a section of fence. They rode to where the land began to rise into the foot of a towering peak. The fence was new. The cedar posts still held the yellow, new look and the strands of barb wire glittered in the sun.

"We strung this piece last week," said Dean as they rode along the perimeter of the fence. "This was all open range until the trouble started."

"What is the trouble anyway?" asked Quinton. He liked this freckled, red-haired youth. He was about the only hand on Anchor that Quinton approved of. The others were hard, calloused men.

Dean laid a searching glance on Quinton. The youth's mouth tightened. It was as though he were trying to make up his mind as to how far he could trust Quinton.

"The boss claims the small outfits are robbing him," Dean said, voice soft with caution. "He says they rustle his cattle. Some of them also filed on a piece of ground that Anchor had always claimed as its own but it was never registered. The boss wants that land back—and some more besides."

Out of some trees on the other side of the fence a rider emerged. Dean reined in his sorrel quickly, tense and wary all at once. Quinton halted the black. He saw the rider come to an abrupt stop on sighting them.

Tension and hostility lay between them like a tangible thing. Quinton glanced at Dean and saw that the youth's face was hard but also a little sad. A long while the three men sat frozen on their halted mounts, staring without the exchange of a word. Finally, the rider stirred. Carefully, he turned his horse and rode back into the trees.

Bucky Dean sighed. A faint disgust showed in the shape of his mouth. "I know that fellow," he said. "Me and him used to chum around. Ben Sawtelle. Many's the time we got drunk together in Gunsight on Saturday nights. Now we don't even talk to each other any more. I suppose one of these days we might even swap lead." He sounded bitter.

"I take it you don't like Anchor," Quinton said softly.

Dean's hand swiveled sharply as he laid a keen look on Quinton. "What do you mean by that?"

Quinton shrugged. "You don't sound very happy."

"Do you blame me when a shooting war is ready to break out any minute?"

"Is it as bad as that?"

"It's been building up to it a long time. It almost started the other day when you helped Mrs. Gillenwater. It's a good thing she wasn't hurt."

"What did she do to get Red Armour and the others after her?" Quinton asked.

Dean's brows went up. "Don't you know?"

"She never told me and I didn't ask."

"She sneaked on to Keyhole and cut a brand new fence Red Armour had just built. She cut it all to hell. Armour built it to keep Anchor cattle from using a spring. That's some of the land that used to belong to Anchor. Years ago somebody got the legal descriptions mixed up when they were registered and that's how Anchor lost the ground."

"When was the mistake found out?"

The ground sloped here and the horses moved, side by side, at a walk. Bucky Dean took out the makin's and rolled a cigarette. He rocked easily in the saddle, not spilling a single flake of tobacco. He offered the sack to Quinton but Quinton shook his head.

"It was common knowledge when I went to work for Anchor five years ago." Dean paused to lick the paper. "The Colonel didn't mind, though. He said Anchor was big enough and that there was land enough for everybody. The Colonel was a good man to work for. The White Peaks was a good range while he was alive. Then he died and his son took over. Things have been getting worse ever since."

"Why do you stay on at Anchor then?"

Dean seemed absorbed in profound reflection. After a while, he said gravely, "Anchor's my outfit. I went to work for it when I was just fifteen years old. It's the only outfit I've ever worked for. While the Colonel was alive I'd have ridden through hell and high water for it. I'd quit this minute except that Anchor's my outfit. I wouldn't know where else to go. I'm not happy at Anchor but I wouldn't be happy anywhere else either." He paused as if thinking on something, then he shrugged. "I keep hoping that things will change and be like the old days again. I know better, but I just can't help myself. Anchor's my outfit, Quinton."

"Has there been any rough stuff so far?" Quinton asked.

Dean was riding with his head bowed a little. He lifted it now and appeared to stare off at a luminous bank of white clouds building up above the White Peaks. "No one's been killed yet," he said with a touch of bitterness. "There's been a little fence-cutting but mostly it's been words. The only shots fired were those at Mrs. Gillenwater. Red Armour's a hot-head. If he'd creased her, all hell would have busted loose. The boss is just waiting for an excuse to turn Dalhart and his curly wolves loose." His mouth twisted in a wry grin. "You didn't do such a good turn after all, Quinton—not for Clay Gillenwater, any way."

"Maybe things will work out," said Quinton.

Dean turned his head and laid a dubious look on Quinton. "Not after what Gillenwater's done lately."

"What's that?"

"I heard it tossed around in the bunkhouse a week ago. The small outfits had a tough winter and most of them had to borrow money from the bank. Gillenwater bought up some notes that Bar H Bar, Keyhole and Flying W owe. He's given them two weeks to pay or he takes over."

"That would be legal, wouldn't it?" said Quinton. "Those outfits knew what they were signing."

Dean shook his head. "They signed because the bank had always agreed to extensions in the past. Then Gillenwater stepped in. He's the biggest depositor in the bank and he said he'd take his business somewhere else. Anyway, he buffaloed the bank and they sold him the notes and now he's turned around and put the pressure on every one else that might loan Wes Hawthorne, Red Armour and Pete Corey the money. The boss is a big man in these parts, Quinton. He throws a lot of weight around." He shook his head again. "Either way, hell is sure to bust loose. Those boys won't stand for losing their ranches. Legal or not, they'll fight to get their land back. And if they manage to dig up the money somewhere, then Gillenwater will turn Dalhart loose." He paused and laid a slightly narrowed look on Quinton. "Didn't Dalhart send for you?"

"I never knew the man until the other day."

Dean's glance drifted to Quinton's gun. "I can't make you out," said the youth. "You've been around. I can see that. But you're not Dalhart's stripe. Just what are you doing on Anchor?"

"I was broke and needed a job."

"You couldn't have needed one that bad."

Quinton was thinking of the true reason he had hired out to Anchor and now he realized it had only a little to do with Stony Brice. It left him feeling grave and even regretful.

"Every man makes mistakes, Bucky," he said. "Sometimes I think I make more than my share . . ."

Chapter 4

That night one of Anchor's riders brought word that the small ranchers had started a roundup. It was not shipping season but the motive behind the beef gather was apparent to everyone. An air heavy with tension and ominousness settled over the place.

Quinton and Bucky Dean sat on a wagon tongue down by the corrals, apart from the other men who were grouped in and around the bunkshack. Daylight was failing. The highest crests of the mountains were still red from the dying sun but in the valleys shadows were thickening.

Quinton sat quietly, drawing on his after-supper cigarette and watching Dalhart who stood just outside the bunkhouse entrance conversing with Slim Sunderland and George Marberry. They were gun-hung men as hard as Dalhart.

Beside Quinton, Bucky Dean stirred restlessly. The youth had a cigarette in his mouth and he seemed to be deriving no pleasure from it. When it was only half-smoked he dropped it to the ground and stamped it out with a vicious, angry twist of his heel.

Dalhart broke away from Marberry and Sunderland now and strode toward the house.

When the ramrod disappeared inside, young Dean said, "This is where it starts." His voice sounded old and bitter.

Compassion for this youth, torn between loyalty and a sense of wrongness, filled Quinton. "Maybe it's nothing," he said soothingly.

"Nothing?" Dean snorted. "You know why Hawthorne, Armour and the others are holding that roundup, don't you? It's to get the money to pay off those notes they owe to the boss. Do you think that will stop him? I've got a month's pay that says Dalhart talks the boss into riding against Bar H Bar and the others tonight."

"Save your money, Bucky," said Quinton. "I've got Clay Gillenwater figured out as a man who likes to think things out before he does anything. He's not the kind to go off half-cocked."

"Dalhart's been spoiling for a fight ever since he came to Anchor a year ago."

"Who runs Anchor? Dalhart or Gillenwater?"

Young Dean was silent. He stared gloomily at the ground, hands clasped between his knees.

The door of the big house opened and Dalhart came out. He paused on the gallery as if someone had spoken to him from inside. A moment later Clay Gillenwater emerged and he and Dalhart stood framed in the lamplight spilling through the open door. They conversed quietly for a while. Then Dalhart stepped down to the ground and started for the bunkhouse.

Sunderland and Marberry had been joined by Frio Bates and the three stepped ahead to intercept Dalhart. Sunderland asked something quietly and Dalhart stopped and made an angry gesture with his palms turned up. Then he brushed past Sunderland and stalked into the bunkhouse.

"Looks like you were wrong, Bucky," Quinton said softly. "Anchor's not riding tonight."

"There will be other nights," the youth said gloomily.

I'm afraid you're right, Quinton thought.

Three days later, Quinton and Dean rode northward. They worked up into high country beyond Anchor's boundary and then swung back, riding as much as they could through timber and avoiding sight of any ranch buildings.

At noon they reined in their mounts in a grove of aspens and dismounted to get the saddle stiffness out of their bones. It was a warm, pleasant day. The sun slanted through the trees here and there, making small patterns of light on the otherwise shadowed ground.

The silence of the high country was all about them as they chewed on some jerky. Neither man had spoken much that day. Quinton felt somber and reflective. He had been trying all morning to figure a way out of his dilemma but had been unable to arrive at any satisfactory conclusion. Now and then his mind formed a brief image of

Kate Gillenwater and this also added to the disturbance roiling his mind.

Young Bucky Dean stared moodily at the trees directly in front of him but it was apparent that he was not seeing them. There was something troubling him, too. It showed in the grave, pensive cast of his mouth.

After some time Dean roused himself and looked at Quinton. "Where do you think they're holding the herd?" the youth asked.

Quinton shrugged. "You know the country better than I do, Bucky."

Dean swore with vehemence and disgust. "This is a hell of a note," he declared. "You know what will happen if we spot that herd and report its location to Dalhart?"

"Maybe it won't be us that finds it," said Quinton, feeling a little sorry for young Dean. "There are six of us out looking for it."

"You were right about Gillenwater," said the youth. "You can tell he's waiting for them to get all their beef together before doing anything about it. He's gonna wait to scatter them until they won't have the time to round them up again and meet the deadline he's set for payment. You were right about him not going off half-cocked, Riley."

Riding on, they came to a flashing creek that was shallow enough to be forded. When they reached the opposite bank, a rider popped out of some cedars. It was Ben Sawtelle. There was a rifle in his hands and the weapon was trained on Quinton and Dean.

Dean reined in his mount with a sharp gasp of surprise. For an instant he looked stunned, then he was suddenly shamed and ill at ease. Quinton looked from the bore of the rifle at Ben Sawtelle's eyes and saw only a deadly determination there.

Sawtelle sent his bay ahead slowly and carefully so that a sudden lurch might not spoil the bead he had drawn on Quinton and Dean. Sawtelle looked not much older than Dean. Sawtelle's face was burned red by the sun and he had a wide, clear countenance that now was tense with resolve.

Quinton folded his hands over the horn. Bucky Dean had raised his right hand somewhat, indicating that he had no intention of going for his gun. There was pain in the youth's eyes.

Sawtelle halted the bay. The rifle pointed mostly at Quinton but Sawtelle's glance was more on Dean. Sawtelle, too, appeared disturbed and unhappy.

"Kind of strayed from your cavvy, ain't you, Bucky?" asked Ben Sawtelle.

Dean could not speak. He lowered his head in a quick nod and then kept it down while he stared at the ground.

"What are you looking for?" asked Sawtelle.

Again Dean did not speak.

Quinton said, "Strays."

"I didn't ask you nothing," said Sawtelle, his voice abruptly hard and vicious. His eyes glowed with hate as he held them on Quinton a moment. Then Sawtelle's glance swung back to Dean and it was troubled and sad again. "You know you should stay on your side of the fence, Bucky."

Dean raised his head now. He still looked uncomfortable. "What you aiming to do, Ben?"

"If it was any one but you, Bucky, I'd take you in to the boss." Sawtelle sounded miserable.

"We didn't mean no harm, Ben."

"Who's your partner?"

"Riley Quinton."

"Quinton?" said Sawtelle, his brows going up. A look of bitter hate tightened the skin on his cheeks. His rifle moved so that the bore pointed directly at Quinton's heart. Sawtelle seemed to forget about Bucky Dean. "So you're Quinton," Sawtelle said, mouthing the words contemptuously, "the Texas gunslinger who tried to spy on Bar H Bar. I think Stony Brice would like to see you, Quinton. I think he would like to see you very much."

Quinton's heart went cold. In the yawn of the rifle bore he could see death staring at him.

"He didn't mean no harm, Ben," cried Dean. "Quinton's all right. You've got him all wrong. He's not like Dalhart and the others."

"You ride on, Bucky," said Sawtelle, his lips stiff, his glance steady on Quinton. "For old times' sake, you ride on. But I'm taking Quinton in."

"I give you my word Quinton is all right."

"I've got my orders," said Sawtelle. "I should take you in, too, but I'll pretend you never got on our side of the fence. I'll pretend that this time, Bucky, but never again. So ride on out while you've got the chance."

"I'll ride if Quinton comes with me."

"You'll ride alone," said Sawtelle, eyes still locked with Quinton's.

"Look at me, Ben."

Quinton saw startlement distend Sawtelle's eyes briefly. Even before Sawtelle shifted his glance he seemed to know what he would see. Surprise gave way to dismay on Sawtelle's features and then wrath colored the long planes of his cheeks.

"Look at me," Bucky Dean said again.

Defiantly but also reluctantly Sawtelle turned his glance on Dean. Bitterness edged the corners of Sawtelle's mouth when he saw the drawn .44 Remington in Bucky Dean's hand. The .44 was aimed at Ben Sawtelle's belly.

"Quinton's coming with me, Ben," said Dean. His voice was sad and regretful.

Sawtelle's hands tightened where they held the rifle until his knuckles showed white. The barrel drooped a little, then started to rise again in a burst of angry rebellion.

"Don't make me kill you, Ben!" Dean cried out, voice shrill and taut.

A look of pain came to Sawtelle's eyes. Abruptly the fight went out of him. When he spoke his voice was thick with hurt and disgust. "So you'd kill me to save the hide of a dirty, back-shooting gunslinger? All right, Bucky," he said bitterly, dropping the rifle to the ground. "You've called the game but the hand isn't over yet. And let me tell you this. You better kill me now, Bucky, because the next time I see you I'm drawing on you. Is that clear? You're all Anchor now. You've grown mean and dirty like the rest of Anchor. So you better kill me now because, so help me, I'm killing you the first chance I get!"

Anchor rode four nights later. They rode in two groups, one led by Clay Gillenwater, the other by Dalhart. Quinton was in Dalhart's band while Bucky Dean rode with Gillenwater. Quinton felt strangely alone without the youth beside him.

When they came to Anchor's fence, they halted while Dalhart dismounted and cut a gap in the wire for them to pass through. Then the two groups parted. The men had been briefed carefully before leaving Anchor and not a word was said as each band struck out by itself.

There was a high wind blowing, scudding a cloud now and then across the face of the moon. They rode alternately in shadow and moonlight.

The only sounds in the night were the squeaking of saddle leather and an occasional ring as a shod hoof struck stone.

The herd was being held on a long plateau. The ground was on the southern flank of Flying W, right next to Keyhole. Dalhart avoided coming anywhere near Keyhole's buildings and Anchor's men reached the plateau without incident. Clusters of trees dotted the plateau and Dalhart led his men through these for cover. At the edge of one of these groves, Dalhart held up a hand, halting his men.

The waiting began then. When the moon came out, they could see a long way across the plateau, almost to where it ended abruptly at the edge of a precipice two miles away. Then a cloud would cover the moon and the surface of the plateau would be black with concealing shadow.

One of the men built a smoke and struck a match. Dalhart wheeled his horse as the tiny flame flared and brought the back of his hand smashing across the rider's face. The rider groaned and almost went pitching out of his kak. Dalhart said not a word.

Quinton waited, full of distaste and disgust. What portended was something that went violently against his instincts and nature. He contemplated the small of Dalhart's back as the Anchor ramrod sat his roan ahead of the group. It took all of Quinton's restraint to keep from challenging Dalhart and then shooting him down.

Then a thought struck Quinton. Brice would be with the herd. Perhaps an opportunity would present itself for him to take Brice. There would be a lot of confusion and if he should encounter Brice he could take the killer or shoot him down if Brice resisted, and thus the long vigil would be over for Quinton. He could then start back to Texas, away from the hate and viciousness and greed that were so rampant here in the White Peaks. He was just beginning to feel a little more at ease because of this line of thinking when the first shots broke out.

They were faint with distance but the waiting men perked up. A hush, awesome and ominous, seemed to settle over the land as they waited, scarcely breathing, for what was to follow.

Then it came.

At first it was only a rumble, like the far-off roll of thunder. At the moment, it suggested nothing that was menacing or frightening. The men, however, tensed in their saddles. Dalhart raised a hand and kept it there, shoulder-high. His head was cocked to one side as he listened with a cruel and eager pleasure.

Quinton had to clench his teeth to keep from cursing aloud. He slid his .44 from its holster but he was not the only one with a pistol in his hand. Quinton's eyes were slits as he glared at Dalhart's back. A great and violent fury pawed at the edges of Quinton's brain. His thumb caressed the hammer-spur and once he drew it back to full cock with the barrel pointing at Dalhart's back but at the last instant he checked himself. Half fearfully, he glanced around to see if any one had noticed but the others were too intent on the approaching stampede.

The sound of it was swelling. It grew in volume until it seemed it would fill the space between earth and sky with its senseless, cacophonous fury. Even the ground shuddered under the pound of the maddened, terrified hoofs. The clacking of horns was sharp and distinct above all the other uproar.

A cloud passed from the face of the moon and Quinton saw them then. They burst over a rise with a sudden, chilling appearance and came hurtling on, a dark, serpentine mass of speeding destruction and death.

Dalhart turned his head as he addressed his men. His shrill words echoed above the tumult of the stampede. "Over the cliff they go. Every goddam one of them!"

Dalhart threw back his head as he emitted a shrill rebel yell. His arm came down and the men set spurs to their horses.

The stampeding cattle were veering for the trees but Anchor's men rode at them, discharging their pistols. Gun thunder added to the din. The night was streaked with long lances of gun flame. The gunshots penetrated through the terror of the leaders and they swung back, away from the trees, straight for the precipice at the end of the plateau.

Quinton paid only passing attention to the cattle. He let all the riders get ahead of him. He reined the black to the left, in the direction from which the cattle had come. Another cloud blocked off the moon and Quinton cursed.

He rode cautiously, not knowing what he would find. The night made every man an enemy. Even if a rider should loom up out of darkness he could not know whether the man belonged to Anchor or to Bar H Bar and its confederates.

There was more gun roar behind him. That would be Dalhart and the others as they kept the herd headed for the precipice. There were also gun shots from the other side of the herd and suddenly part of it broke away. A veritable fusillade across the way startled a bunch of steers out of their headlong flight to the cliff and sent them charging at Quinton.

He had to forget Brice now. He wheeled the black and spurred it into a frantic run for a bunch of trees that loomed up blackly against the skyline. There were more gun shots and the cattle veered again. Quinton, looking back over his shoulder, saw the riders then.

There were four of them and they were trying

to get this small bunch of cattle to circling. This appeared to be all that would be saved from the herd. One of the riders spotted Quinton fleeing and threw a shot at him. The bullet whined above Quinton's head and then the black was in the trees.

He reined in the black. Breath was hot and labored in Quinton's throat, sweat stained his brow and trickled down into his eyes. There was no doubt that those riders were not Anchor men else they would not be trying to save the cattle. Was Stony Brice one of the four?

Quinton's heart quickened. He wanted so much to get the long hunt over with that he cursed softly with irritable impatience. He edged the black out of the trees. Guns were exploding near and far as various groups of riders tangled. The cloud left the moon again and the four riders spotted Quinton.

They shouted in rage and rancor and three of them came at him, guns roaring. He jumped the black back into the trees. Leaden slugs made ugly, whistling noises as they clipped twigs and needles off the pine branches all about him. He waited, hunched forward in the kak, watching them come through a break in the trees.

The moon was bright at this moment and Quinton was almost sure one of them was Brice when another cloud dimmed the moonlight and then it cut off completely. He sat there, trembling with anger and helplessness. He wanted only Brice. He had no desire to kill anyone else, but in the darkness he could not be sure even of Brice.

Quinton gritted his teeth and waited. He wanted to wait until they were real close but a slug plucked at his shirt sleeve and he realized he could wait no longer, not unless he did not care whether he lived or died.

He raised his .44 and threw two quick shots at them. Someone cried out. There was pain in the cry and Quinton's heart went cold. Was that Brice, or some innocent? He tried telling himself it was either him or them but he found small consolation in the thought.

Suddenly he realized he could not do it this way. As much as he wanted to take Brice, he could not bring himself to risk killing someone against whom he bore no ill will. Swearing savagely, Quinton wheeled the black and spurred it into a headlong run.

Branches clawed at his thighs and arms. Once he got one across the face in a stinging swipe that ripped a cry out of him and almost knocked him out of the saddle. He had to grab the horn with both hands and keep his seat. His eyes were wet with tears of pain.

Behind him he could hear them in pursuit. He urged the black on faster. The trees thinned a little and the black put on a burst of speed as it thundered down a slope. It broke out of the trees into open ground and Quinton turned the black's head in the direction of Anchor.

He had a swift horse with a lot of stamina and Quinton exulted as the black began to pull away. The moon came out again and, glancing back, he saw the three riders falling behind. One of them tried a couple of shots but they fell short.

He did not slow the black until he had reached the gap in Anchor's fence. The black was blowing hard now, its stride faltering now and then. When Quinton finally pulled it in on Anchor ground, the black stood on straddled legs, head hanging while its lathered flanks heaved.

Two riders approached. In the darkness Quinton could not recognize them. Drawing his gun, he waited for them to come up. They reined in sharply when they spied Quinton. For the moment, recognition eluded them also.

Then one of them said, "Is that you, Quinton?"

Relief flowed through Quinton. "It's me," he said. These were two of the men who had ridden out with Dalhart. Somehow, Quinton was a little disappointed. He had been hoping one of them would be Bucky Dean. He was worried about the youth. He would be worried until Dean showed up alive and well.

The riders came ahead and Quinton holstered his gun. Together they rode into Anchor.

They were the first ones to return. The cook had not gone to bed. He had two large pots of coffee boiling and Quinton and the other two helped themselves. However, the coffee did not soothe Quinton. As the time wore on, he grew more and more nervous thinking of Bucky Dean.

Quinton went out into the night. He built a cigarette and lighted it. Up in the big house lights were burning in some of the windows and all at once he found himself thinking of Kate Gillenwater instead of Dean. The thoughts disgusted Quinton and he swore viciously. He walked over to the corrals and stood with his back to the house.

Riders began to drift in. Some came in singly, some in pairs. Once a group of four rode in together. Quinton studied them all, his heart rapid and cold in his breast, but Bucky Dean was not among them. A feeling of dread descended on Quinton.

Two more riders came and one of them was Dalhart. The ramrod spied Quinton standing there and Dalhart walked over. For a while he stood there silent, staring fixedly at Quinton.

Then Dalhart said, "You got through pretty quick, Quinton." The tone was flat, hostile.

Anger stirred in Quinton. He was thinking that there undoubtedly had been dying tonight but those who deserved it were still alive. It made him feel mean and ugly.

"Did you expect me to stop and count coup?" he said sharply.

Dalhart's head flung up in an irate gesture. In the darkness Quinton could feel the naked hate in the ramrod's eyes. "I told you once I don't like smart answers, Quinton."

"I don't care what you like."

"So?" said Dalhart, purring. A spur tinkled as he shifted his weight. "You're talking tough, Quinton."

"I can back it up." He wanted something harsh to take the disgust and the worry from his mind. He did not care if this something meant shooting it out with Dalhart.

This hardness in Quinton's tone and attitude prompted Dalhart to make another consideration. He was silent a while, a slender, mean-eyed little man, his thinking vicious and as secret as the shadows of the night.

After a pause, Dalhart said, "You didn't ride with us when we went after the herd." His voice was not so sharp any more, but it was still cold and unfriendly. "Why?"

"You wanted all the cows over the cliff, didn't you? I saw those riders trying to head off part of the herd and I rode there to try to break it up but they were four to one." He paused. He was still angry and spoiling for trouble inside. "You got any complaint about that?"

Dalhart did not speak right away. He appeared to be running something through his mind. Finally he said, "I don't like you, Quinton. I

74

don't like your ways. I want you to remember that it wasn't me who hired you on at Anchor. If I had my way, I'd send you packing right this minute, but that's something I can't do." He paused and sucked in an audible breath. It sounded like he was trying to contain himself. "I'm keeping my eyes on you, Quinton. The first funny move you make I'm cutting down on you. Is that clear?"

"Any time, Dalhart," Quinton said through his teeth. "Any time."

Sudden fury ran naked through Dalhart's tone. "Do you think that if I had any choice I'd be putting it off?" he snarled, voice quivering with rage. "I'd draw on you right now!"

Before Quinton could say anything, Dalhart turned and strode off angrily toward the bunk-house. Three riders came in now and Quinton forgot Dalhart and looked them over. One was Clay Gillenwater. Neither of the other two was Bucky Dean.

Dean did not ride in until an hour later. Quinton had begun to give up hope when a lone rider loomed up out of the darkness and it was Dean. Quinton wanted to cry out but something lodged in his throat. He watched mutely as the youth rode up and dismounted.

The instant Dean was on the ground he sagged up against his horse, his face pressed against the saddle. He's hurt, Quinton thought, and ran up to the youth. The instant Quinton touched him Dean straightened with an almost spasmodic abruptness. He started to strike out but then Dean saw that it was Quinton and the youth froze with his arm raised.

A moment he was like that. Then a sob racked him and his arm dropped and his shoulders slumped. "I'm beat, Riley. I'm dead beat."

An air of exuberance lay over Anchor the next morning. After Anchor's riders had compared notes, it was deduced that most of the herd lay dead at the bottom of the precipice. The few cows that remained alive would not provide Wes Hawthorne and the others with enough money to pay off Clay Gillenwater's note. Thus the victory was Anchor's and Anchor's men gloried coarsely and raucously in their triumph.

Quinton could not stand the rough horseplay and loud hilarity of the bunkhouse and he went outside as soon as he was dressed. Bucky Dean went also but the youth was not talking this morning, not even to Quinton. Dean's face looked troubled and sad and he went off by himself. Quinton did not try to follow.

He saw Clay Gillenwater come out of the big house with a swagger and walk down to the corrals where he was met by Dalhart. Gillenwater handed the ramrod a cigar and then the two men lit up. They conversed a while and then both laughed heartily. The sound of that laughter made Quinton sick to his stomach.

One of the corrals held half a dozen wild broncos that had been brought in from the range. Dalhart came over to Quinton and ordered him to start breaking the horses. Then Dalhart gave the rest of the hands the day off. Quinton knew he was being castigated for what he had said to Dalhart the night before. Instead of resentment, Quinton experienced a wry pleasure. The work would keep him occupied and give his mind something else to think about.

Most of the hands rode in to Gunsight but some stayed behind at Anchor in the event that the small ranchers might try retaliation. After a while, Bucky Dean drifted down to the corral where Quinton was working. The youth began giving Quinton a hand. Dean made very little conversation and Quinton did not try to pry. The youth still looked troubled and shaken.

That afternoon, Quinton had knocked off for a smoke when he saw the rider coming toward Anchor. Clay Gillenwater, too, spied the horseman and Anchor's owner left the house and walked down to the corrals to intercept the rider who was Luke Fowler.

Fowler rode up as straight in the saddle as a young man. He reined in his buckskin beside Quinton but Fowler did not so much as glance that way. His eyes had picked up Clay Gillenwater and had never left him. Fowler's white mustache bristled with forcibly contained anger.

Gillenwater was puffing on a cigar. He let the smoke dribble up in front of his face and through the haze he watched Fowler with ill-concealed amusement. This attitude seemed to infuriate Fowler all the more.

"You think you've won, don't you, Clay?" Fowler said through his teeth. His voice trembled with wrath. "You think all you've got to do is wait a few more days and then take over Bar H Bar and Keyhole and Flying W. Is that what you're so happy about?"

"Now, now, Luke," Gillenwater said soothingly. "There's nothing for you to get so smoked up about."

"Isn't there?" Fowler cried, mouth tight with rage. One hand rose and balled in a fist. It looked like he would bring it down on Gillenwater's head but then Fowler got hold of himself. His chest swelled as he took a deep breath and his fingers uncurled slowly and reluctantly and then his arm dropped. "I've heard of some dirty, lowdown things in my time, Clay, but what you did last night was the dirtiest, sneakiest of them all. You're a stink on the face of the earth, Clay!"

Gillenwater's features spasmed in a sudden burst of wrath. The mocking amusement fled from him. He looked hot and brutal now.

"Watch your tongue, Luke," he said sharply.

"I'm about through taking your preachments. Watch your tongue or, so help me, I'll make you wish you'd never opened your yap at me!"

"What do you want me to do?" cried Fowler. "Congratulate you for what you did last night?"

"What are you crying about? There were none of your cows in that herd."

"That's not enough to buy me off." Fowler leaned forward in his saddle. He bent down until his face was directly in front of Gillenwater's. "Listen to me, Clay," Fowler said, his voice so wrathful it could scarcely rise above a hoarse whisper. "Listen to me good. Your notes are paid off, Clay. This afternoon Wes Hawthorne and Red Armour and Pete Corey rode to the bank in Gunsight and there they've deposited a check big enough to cover what they owe you. Do you want to know who wrote them that check? It was me! Do you hear, Clay? Me!"

A strangled roar burst out of Gillenwater. He reached up and, grabbing hold of Fowler by the lapels of his jacket, he jerked the old man out of the saddle. Fowler squalled in alarm and made a pass at his .44 Starr but by this time he was out of the kak and hurtling earthward and his frantic fingers missed the handle of the gun. Fowler hit the ground so hard that the impact smashed him down on his knees. With another hard, vicious jerk, Gillenwater pulled the old man to his feet.

Gillenwater's face was suffused with rage. His

mouth worked, his eyes glared, muscles writhed and leaped in his neck. "I told you to stay out of it," he shouted hoarsely. "Now, damn you, you'll pay for it!"

Gillenwater's hand was raised to smash Fowler across the face when Quinton leaped. He came in behind Gillenwater and he caught Gillenwater's arms and with a violent pull he broke Gillenwater's grip on Fowler. Gillenwater snarled in thwarted rage. He arched his back in an attempt to dislodge Quinton's hold but Quinton had his arms clasped around the big man's chest. Quinton's fingers were locked together and he gave another jerk that almost sent Gillenwater to his knees. The man cursed savagely. He jabbed back with a spur, seeking Quinton's thigh, but Quinton took a step back, quickly, pulling Gillenwater down a little, and then Quinton raised a knee and jammed it up against the small of Gillenwater's back.

He was holding Gillenwater like that when he heard Fowler cry out and then something crashed against the side of Quinton's head. He knew a flash of pain and a wave of engulfing blackness came hurtling down on him but it did not quite reach him. He saw the ground come up, seeking his face, and he threw his arms out in front of him and he got them between the ground and his face just in time. Even so the jolt seemed to knock most of the breath out of him.

He groaned and rolled over and then some inner urgency brought him up on his knees. His head was clearing. His eyes stung with pain but he could see and now all the disgust and resentment that had been building up in him ever since he had come to Anchor burst out of him in an angry rush of words as he saw Dalhart standing there, gun drawn and aimed at him.

"Go on and shoot, you yellow-bellied bastard," cried Quinton. "You've been spoiling for it ever since I came to Anchor. Well, now's your chance. My gun's in the bunkhouse. There's no risk in it for you. These are the kind of odds you like, aren't they? Go on and shoot. You've never had the guts to give a man an even break!"

Dalhart's chest swelled as he took a prodigious breath. His knuckles showed white from the force of his grip on the .45. Rage and hate and the craving to kill glowered luminously in his eyes. His thumb racked back the hammer of the .45.

Then Clay Gillenwater stepped between Quinton and Dalhart's ready .45. The wrath was gone from Gillenwater. He had himself in hand although an aftermath of his ire still showed in the tint on his cheeks.

"Let it pass, Dalhart," Gillenwater said. "I lost my head. I'd have killed Luke if Quinton hadn't jumped me. Let it pass."

Dalhart was quivering with rage. "No one can talk like that to me," he cried. He reached out a hand to brush Gillenwater aside. "Stand back. I'm killing the dirty son!"

"Yes, Clay, stand back," said Luke Fowler, and something in his tone swung Dalhart's and Gillenwater's glances swiftly to him. "Let Dalhart try to shoot an unarmed man. That's all I need to make me put a bullet in his stinking heart!"

Fowler stood there, the big Starr cocked and ready in his hand. The bore pointed at Dalhart's chest. When Dalhart saw this and the look on Fowler's face, Dalhart blanched. The fury went out of him. His arm relaxed and his .45 lowered.

"Go on, Dalhart," said Fowler. "There are too many Texas gunmen on Anchor anyway. No one will miss you. Go on and shoot Quinton."

Dalhart's mouth punched with mortification and helpless anger. His head bowed and he glared at the ground. Without a word, he holstered his .45, and then he stood there, lean and tense and aquiver with wrath, his white-knuckled hands bunched into fists.

Now that the situation was in hand, Quinton rose to his feet. On the instant, he felt a little shaky but the sensation began to pass. His head ached where Dalhart's gun barrel had slammed it. Other than that, Quinton felt all right.

Fowler went over to his buckskin and mounted. He still held the Starr in his hand. He kept it there even after he was in the saddle. He stared down at Clay Gillenwater with a mixture of compassion and pity.

"Why don't you let everything be, Clay?" Fowler said gently, all the animosity gone from his tone. "Men died last night. Five hundred steers are dead at the foot of a cliff. Think on that, will you, Clay? Think on it and then call an end to it. Will you do that for old times' sake, Clay?"

"You've picked your side, Luke. Don't come bawling to me when the sky falls on you."

Fowler sighed. For an instant, his face hardened, then it was said with pity again. "The sky can fall on you, too, Clay. Have you ever thought of that?"

Without waiting for Gillenwater's reply, Fowler touched spurs to the buckskin. As he rode past Quinton, Fowler ducked his head briefly in a gesture of thanks. Then he was going, old and straight in the saddle but heavy and sick at heart . . .

Chapter 5

The sun was at high noon when Quinton decided to call a break. He was riding fence all alone today and he was at the north end of Anchor where the land began to merge with the first monstrous rise of a towering peak. He had not seen a rider since he had left the ranch at dawn that morning.

He reined in the black at the edge of a bank of pines. A cold breeze was sweeping down off the mountain but the trees broke it here and with the sun directly overhead it was warm and comfortable. While the black grazed, Quinton sat on a stone and built a cigarette. While he was smoking, he saw the horse's head suddenly fling up, ears perked. Then the black whinnied and an answer came from above.

Quinton's first instinct was to grab the handle of his gun, then he saw the rider coming down the slope and Quinton froze as he was. Dryness rasped his throat and then the ache came, small and poignant.

She was wearing a gray Stetson but the ends of her bronze hair hung down her shoulders and the sun found red fire there. The palomino's hide

84

shone like yellow gold and the ornate silver-work on bridle and saddle flashed glitteringly where the beams of sunlight struck it.

She pulled in the palomino in front of Quinton. She sat slim and straight in the saddle, looking down at him. The wide brim of her hat shaded the upper half of her face so that he could not read the expression in her eyes. Her mouth, however, looked grave and even sad.

They did not speak for a minute. They just stared at each other. Quinton took his hand off his gun. The pain in his throat was very sharp now. He was aware of the pattern of her breasts under the plaid shirt and the snug fit of the Levi's over her hips.

The black came over and nuzzled the palomino. Then both horses put their heads down and began to graze. The woman's stare broke now. She swung a leg lithely over the cantle of her saddle and stepped down.

"Do you have a cigarette, Quinton?" she said. Her voice was low and throaty, like he had remembered it so many times in the loneliness of his nights.

Without answering her, he took out the makin's and began to build a smoke. He gave all his attention to this but he was aware that she was studying him intently. It would have made him very happy except that he kept thinking that she was another man's wife.

When he was through, he rose to his feet and handed her the cigarette. "Aren't you having one?" she asked.

He shook his head and struck a match. She ducked her face as he held the flame to her cigarette and he had a whiff of peach blossoms that stuck cloyingly in his nostrils.

She blew out a cloud of smoke that hesitated a moment in front of her face. Her head was thrown back a little as she looked up at him. He could see the color of her eyes now. They were a pale, gold-flecked green.

"Why do you stay on at Anchor, Quinton?" she asked.

The question startled him so that he could not answer immediately. He could tell her the truth, he thought, but he did not consider it proper. So he said:

"I don't know what you mean."

"You haven't been hitting it off so well with Dalhart. Everyone can tell you're not very happy. I should think that under these circumstances any man would quit. Yet you stay on."

His heart hit a hammerstroke. The urge to tell her was strong in him but then she lifted a hand to put the cigarette in her mouth and the sun glinted off the wedding band on her finger. Now he knew disappointment and disgust.

"Where else can I get paid two hundred a month?" he said. His tone was bitter.

"You're not a gunman." She said it with finality and conviction.

"How do you know?"

"You're not like Dalhart or Sunderland or the others. You're hard and you've used a gun but you don't hire it out for pay. It troubles you when you do. Is that why you're not happy at Anchor?"

I'm not happy because of you, he said to himself. I'll never be happy because of you. But aloud he said nothing. He averted his eyes and stared at the ground.

"Why won't you tell me?" she said, placing a hand on his arm. "Why won't you look at me?"

He lifted his eyes slowly. Her head was thrown back a little as she stared up at him. The smooth line of her throat was there in his sight and the cleft in her chin. Her mouth was parted. He could see the even whiteness of her teeth.

Reaching out, he grabbed her by the arms. He was impulsive and rough and he saw shock strain her face. Pulling her toward him, he bruised his mouth down on hers. He felt her tense and begin to resist. On the instant her lips were cold and unresponsive. In some strange way this made him glad. In this moment his mind told him it was for the best. There really was nothing for him here. She would resist and break away and that would be the end of it.

In the midst of this conviction, he felt fire come into her mouth. Her arms went around him and amazed him with the strength and fierceness of her embrace. Her hand rose and the nails dug into the back of his neck. Now he knew nothing, only the essence that was her, this and an insight of doom which, strangely, he welcomed.

When she finally took her mouth away, she lay limply against him, supported by his arms. Her head was still thrown back. The green eyes burned brightly. The skin was drawn taut over her prominent cheekbones. She was breathing audibly.

After a moment, she got herself in hand. She stood by herself now but she did not pull away from him. She was warm and firm against him.

"Is this why you wouldn't tell me, Quinton?" she asked just above a whisper.

He could not speak. He just nodded.

Moisture glazed her eyes. "Then you know how I felt, too."

"I didn't know," he said. "You never so much as looked at me. You always avoided me."

"Can't you understand why? I was fighting it, Quinton. I'm still fighting it." Her voice broke a little. "What do you think of me, Quinton?"

"What do you mean?"

"I know you think I'm cheap. You think I'm a tramp. Isn't that it?"

"That's not true."

"What else can you think of me?"

"I love you." The words sounded awkward to

him, but he could not think of anything else to say. "I love you."

"How much, Quinton?" she whispered. "How much do you love me?"

"I'm staying on at Anchor," he said. "Someday either Dalhart or your husband will kill me, but I'm staying on."

"Oh, Quinton," she cried, a sob in her voice. She pressed close to him. Her cheek was like velvet against his. He could feel her arms straining with the tightness of her embrace. "Why did it have to happen like this? Why couldn't you have come along two years ago?"

"Would it have made any difference then?" For the moment his tone was cold and bitter.

She perceived this and she took her arms from around his neck and leaned back a little against the cradling of his arms for a searching look of his face. Her eyes were grave and troubled.

"What was I to do, Quinton?" she said, a quaver in her voice. "I put off marrying because I was waiting for the right man to come along. I had never really loved any one and here I was twenty-three years old and still unmarried. Can you blame me for getting a little cynical?

"Then Clay came along. I didn't love him and he didn't love me. He loves only Anchor and power. He wanted a handsome wife and I figured I might as well have money and security if I wasn't to have love. So I married him."

He could not think of anything to say. All that mattered had already been spoken. He loved her and she loved him.

He carried her to the earth with him.

Shadow lay over the buildings of Anchor when Quinton rode in and unsaddled. He ate in the cookshack and then went looking for Bucky Dean.

Dean was sitting on a packing crate behind the barn, his face burrowed in his hands.

"What's wrong, Bucky?"

"Damn you, Riley," the youth cried. "Go on and leave me be!"

Quinton's tone hardened. "Something's eating you, Bucky, and it's no good for you. You've got to snap out of it."

"Yeh," said Dean. He tried a derisive laugh but it came off as more of a sob. "That's easy to say."

"What happened out there that night?"

Dean seemed to press his hands harder against his face. He did not answer.

Quinton took a step ahead. He bent forward a little. "Something happened two nights ago. I knew that when you rode in but I didn't say anything because I thought you'd come out of it. But you haven't. What was it, Bucky?"

"Go away," Dean cried miserably. "Can't you see I don't want to talk about it?"

"You've got to talk about it," said Quinton.

Dean averted his face and kept it like that a while. His breath made ragged sounds as it rasped in and out of his throat. Finally, his head came around and he said:

"I dropped someone that night, Riley. He came at me blazing away and I had no choice. I shot back at him and dropped him."

Quinton released his hold on the youth's wrists and straightened. His eyes were narrowed as he looked down at Dean. "That isn't something that should be taken to heart Bucky. It was either you or him."

"I know," the youth said miserably, "but I just can't feel that way."

"Maybe you didn't kill him," Quinton said gently. "I hit someone, too, but I think I only tagged him. You probably did the same."

"I killed him all right," said Dean. "I could tell from the way he fell out of his saddle. I killed him cold."

"Do you know who it was?"

"No," said Dean, anguish in his voice. "That's what makes it hell, Riley. I didn't stop and look. I just rode away from there. I guess I was afraid to look. Then today I went to Gunsight and there I heard that he was dead." A violent sob racked him. "I'll bet it was me that killed him."

"Who?" asked Quinton.

"Ben Sawtelle."

Chapter 6

There was a tacit understanding between Anchor and the small ranchers that the town of Gunsight was neutral ground. Both factions purchased all their supplies and did their trading in town which was the only settlement of any size in the White Peaks. Thus far all the violence had been restricted to the open range. Nevertheless, an uneasy air hung over Gunsight whenever riders of the two factions were in town.

This Saturday afternoon Quinton rode into Gunsight with a group of Anchor cowboys. He was surprised that Dalhart had not retained him at the ranch for extra duty. For a whole week Dalhart had derived caustic amusement out of assigning Quinton to the most tedious and onerous tasks on the ranch. However, Quinton had grimly accepted each job without audible complaint although rancor and resentment were building up in him.

As Anchor's men rode past the Silver Spur, which was the small rancher's hangout in town, they spotted several ponies at the rack in front of the place. The brands on the ponies were Keyhole, Bar H Bar, Flying W and Windowsash.

Dalhart reined in his sorrel in front of the Palace, which was Anchor's headquarters in

Gunsight. Anchor's men followed suit. They swaggered into the Palace, loud and belligerent in manner, spurs clinking shrilly as boot heels clumped solidly on the hardwood floor.

Quinton was the only one who did not enter the Palace. He paused on the walk and built a cigarette. After he had lighted it, he stood there a while with his back against the front of the building, crinkled eyes looking up and down the main drag through the faint blue of the tobacco smoke which drifted up before his face.

Quinton strolled to the far end of town and then he crossed to the other side of the street and started back. He walked without hurry, immersed in somber thought. He was passing a cafe, his mind full of the bronze-haired woman, when he almost collided with a man coming out. Quinton halted abruptly, head and eyes coming up, and the breath froze in his throat.

The man was Stony Brice.

Two men followed Brice out of the cafe and took up stances one on either side of Brice. Their eyes were bright with hostility.

Brice brushed the open flaps of his jacket aside so that the handles of his twin Remingtons hung free. "So, Quinton," Brice said in his soft, mild way, "you didn't leave the White Peaks."

Anger burned in Quinton but he kept it subdued. It did not show at all in his voice. "That's right," he murmured.

"I hear you're working for Anchor?"

"I am."

The depths of Brice's eyes seemed to have no end. Sun glinted off them. "You didn't take my advice."

"I never said I would."

"You know where this puts you, Quinton. I guess Red Armour was right when he called you an Anchor spy."

"Listen, Brice," Quinton said with a burst of fury that brought Brice's chin tilting up in a show of swift wariness, "you're not ordering me around. Is that clear? I came to hire out to Bar H Bar and you would have none of me. I was looking for work and Anchor hired me. What did you expect me to do—ride the grub line because you don't happen to like the looks of my face? You might run Bar H Bar but you don't run me. I don't have to ask your permission to hire out to anybody."

Brice appeared to withdraw a little. His glance was as expressionless as ever but his manner indicated that he was making a new, thoughtful appraisal of Quinton.

After a short pause, Brice said, "You talk tough."

"Is that something you weren't expecting?" asked Quinton. "Did you think I would turn tail and run?"

"No," Brice said frankly. "You're not the running kind. I can see that." He hesitated as though considering something. "You're not the kind of gunman Anchor has been hiring either. Just why did you come to the White Peaks?"

Quinton's eyes narrowed the barest trifle. "I told you once. I just drifted here."

"You're no drifter." Brice's tone hardened. "Why did you pick the White Peaks when you left Texas?"

"Why did you?" Quinton asked softly.

The question gave Brice pause. The corners of his mouth pulled in again.

"I'm not trying to pick a fight with you," Brice said after a while, "but I'm not running from one if that's what you've got in mind. I don't have anything against you, Quinton, but I want to point out that we're on opposite sides. I'm not trying to order you around when I tell you it would be best if you left the White Peaks. You hang around and someday we'll probably tangle. I can't see any-thing else. Can you?"

No, Quinton thought, I can't, but you don't know the reason yet, Brice, although you're worried a little.

When Quinton did not speak, Brice went on, "Think a little on what I've said to you, Quinton. I hope I never see you again because another time I might not walk off like this."

He turned on his heel and started down the walk, heading for the Silver Spur. His two companions walked behind him. One of them turned and laid a long, hard look on Quinton. Quinton stood there unmoving.

Now he knew the urge to drink. The sense of frustration boiled in him as he headed for the Palace.

Talk died as Quinton pushed through the swing doors. He was aware of this but he paid it no heed. He was too angry with himself to consider anything else. He went up to an open space at the bar and ordered whiskey. He stood there hunched over the bar, a tall, dark man filled with brooding, nagging thoughts. An ugly glitter showed in his eyes. The frame of his lips was cold and mean.

He downed the shot of whiskey and ordered another. Talk had resumed in the Palace but it was only a guarded murmur. Every man's eyes were on Quinton. He was only vaguely conscious of this. His mind was too concerned with the constant thwarting of his plans for him to heed anything else.

He was thinking that he should have called Brice as Brice was walking away. He should have said that he was a deputy from the Trinity and that Brice was under arrest. Then Quinton thought of the two men with Brice and of some more in the Silver Spur. He thought of Anchor's men here in the Palace. Had he tried to take Brice then, the action would have precipitated a pitched battle that undoubtedly would have left several men dead. Quinton cursed softly to himself in vexation.

Spur jingle sounded behind him but Quinton did not turn his head. He stayed hunched over his drink, staring gloomily down at the bar.

Dalhart said, "That was quite a conversation you had with Brice. What did you talk about? The weather?"

Quinton straightened slowly. He had an idea of what was coming and he told himself not to let it get him, but he knew that was going to entail a great effort. He turned even more slowly and saw Dalhart standing there and behind Dalhart were Slim Sunderland and George Marberry.

Quinton said nothing. He took in the amused looks on Sunderland's and Marberry's faces and the goading glitter in Dalhart's eyes. This was getting to be a daily pattern, Quinton thought with annoyance.

Quinton's fists clenched but he forced his fingers to straighten out again. "I thought we weren't supposed to get into trouble in Gunsight."

"Is that what really held you back?" Slim Sunderland said this. He was a tall, gaunt man. His nose came to a sharp point and his mouth was small with prominent front teeth that gave him the look of a beaver. He wore an ivory-handled .45 Colt tied down to his right thigh.

Quinton's eyes were slits as he stared at Sunderland. "I suppose you could have done better?"

Color darkened the skin of Sunderland's cheeks.

"You think I can't take Stony Brice?" he cried.

A cruel humor burned in Quinton. "I don't think you can," he said bluntly. "Not even Brice alone, much less when he has two men with him."

This was a blow to Sunderland's pride. Indignation and wrath deepened the timbre of his tone. "I'll not only take care of Brice," he declared angrily, "but you, too, after I'm done with him."

Sunderland turned and beckoned to an old puncher called Pecos. "You go to the Silver Spur, Pecos, and you tell Stony Brice that if he ain't yellow to meet me in front of Ziebold's Mercantile in exactly fifteen minutes. Just me and Brice alone, no one else to take a hand no matter which one of us drops." Sunderland's eyes swung back to Quinton. Triumph and hate burned in them. "Your turn will come, Quinton."

Dalhart held up a hand as Pecos started to leave and the old puncher stopped. Dalhart stared hard at Slim Sunderland. "You really mean this, Slim?"

Wrath colored Sunderland's features. "You doubting me, too, Dalhart?"

"You know I didn't mean it that way." Dalhart paused. He was thinking on something. "The boss might not like this. He said there was to be no trouble in town."

"This isn't trouble," said Sunderland, eyes bright with an avid, vile anticipation. "This is just between me and Brice. No one else is to take a hand. Just me and Brice." His eyes picked up Quinton again. "Then just me and Quinton."

Dalhart did not speak. He lifted a hand and pulled pensively at his chin. The focus of his eyes was faraway.

"We all know it's Brice holding those ranchers together," Sunderland went on. "Once I drop him you'll see them fall apart. It will be easy pickings then for Anchor. The boss won't be mad, Dalhart." Sunderland's laugh was evil. "Why, he'll wonder why no one thought of it sooner. I bet we'll all get a bonus out of it."

"He's got a point, Dalhart," said George Marberry. He was a short, thick-chested man. Through the black beard rimming his mouth his teeth looked very white. "With Brice dead, you'll see how fast they give up. They'll fall all over themselves in their hurry to get out of the White Peaks. If Slim changes his mind, I'll take on Stony Brice. I think those tied-down Remingtons of his are just a big bluff."

"But will Brice fight?" asked Dalhart.

"He has to," said Sunderland. "He can't back down in front of all the others. After what we did to that herd, he has to fight."

"All right," said Dalhart.

Pecos left the Palace, walking fast . . .

The Silver Spur was down the street from the Palace and on the opposite side. Anchor's men crowded the windows of the Palace. Several of them took up positions in the doorway which provided a better view. Dalhart was one of these and Quinton was another. He was directly behind Dalhart, staring over his shoulder, but the ramrod was so intent on watching that he did not seem to be aware of Quinton.

Ziebold's Mercantile was midway between the Silver Spur and the Palace. Stony Brice was already waiting there. He had removed his jacket and his shirt looked a bright red in the sunlight, as red as fresh blood. He stood there, slight and wiry, looking like a boy who had no business wearing men's clothing and men's weapons. There was no suggestion of menace or deadliness about him now, but Quinton knew that was because Brice was too far away for anyone to see the cruelty in his pale eyes.

Quinton found himself wondering if this was how it had been down on the Trinity but then he remembered that there it had been three to one in a running gunfight and still Brice had come out of it alive. Recalling this made Quinton briefly sorry for Slim Sunderland who was striding toward Brice, arrogant and cocksure.

The sun winked off the ivory handle of Sunderland's .45. His height and confident swagger made Brice seem small and insignificant. The two big Remingtons looked awkward and out-of-place on either side of Brice's hips.

Sunderland came to a halt less than ten feet from Brice. Sunderland inclined a little forward at the waist and the fingers of his right hand crooked beside his holster. Brice did not so much as stir. The only thing that moved about him was the end of his neckerchief which fluttered slightly in the small breeze.

A moment the two froze like that, a tableau of impending violence and death. Life was wrapped up in the fraction of a second, it would take no more than that for one of them to die before the gun of the other. A hush had settled over Anchor's men and Quinton knew it must be like this in the Silver Spur also.

He was thinking that it might have been him out there in place of Sunderland when the two men drew. Sun glinted off blued gun barrels and then the weapons roared. One was the barest echo to the other and for the next few instants it was impossible to tell whose gun had roared first.

Both men stood upright, smoke curling out of the long barrels of their six-shooters. Then Sunderland's .45 dipped a little. His shoulders sagged and he took a step ahead but suddenly there was water in his legs and he went down hard on his knees. The jolt unsettled his Stetson and it rolled off the back of his head. Sunderland started to bend forward but then he caught himself. With an effort he brought his head back up and his .45 lifted.

Brice fired again.

This slug caught Sunderland and hurled him back. He landed on his side with his gun arm under him. His straining, gaping mouth was plain to every man in the Palace. Sunderland kicked twice and then rolled over on his stomach. He did not move after that.

With his left hand, Brice drew his other Remington. He stood in front of Ziebold's, turned so that he faced the Palace. He stood there with a .44-40 in either hand, waiting to see if any of Anchor's men were ready to take up where Slim Sunderland had so abruptly finished.

In the Palace, a couple of riders were cursing in low, bitter tones of disappointment. Quinton could hear Dalhart breathing in front of him but the Anchor ramrod made no move. Several of the men glanced at their foreman, patently awaiting instructions, but Dalhart's stare was fixed on Stony Brice, who still stood facing the Palace. It was apparent that Brice had no chance of escaping alive should Anchor's men open up on him. Brice, however, evinced no fear. There was even a sardonic, angry challenge in the way he stood, a perfect target for anyone in the Palace.

After a while, Brice holstered his weapons and turned. His back was to the Palace as he started toward the Silver Spur. There was no hurry in Brice's steps, he might have been taking a peaceful stroll.

Quinton saw Dalhart's shoulders square and tense. The man's right elbow crooked as his hand lifted. It stopped with the palm brushing the handle of his gun.

"In the back, Dalhart?" Quinton said softly. "Sunderland, at least, had the guts to face Brice fair and square."

Dalhart whirled, mouth twisted in a snarl, eyes blazing. His fingers were clasped tight about the butt of his .45. He looked like he was about to draw but then he saw that Quinton's hand was on his gun, also, and Dalhart froze.

His hate-ridden glance raked Quinton. Dalhart's voice was low and atremble with fury. "Ever since you came to Anchor, Quinton," he said, "you've been trying to make me kill you. Well, I think that day isn't very far off."

Chapter 7

They met where Anchor's line lay against that of Luke Fowler's Broken Bit. There was no fence here out of deference for the old friendship between Colonel Gillenwater and Fowler, but Quinton had heard bunkhouse speculation that the drawing of a fence was not far off. Clay Gillenwater had not forgiven Fowler for loaning money to the small ranchers. To Gillenwater's way of thinking, this had aligned Fowler against Anchor.

The land here was rolling; it was green with graze and clumps of trees. Above, the white crests of the mountains gleamed in the sun. This part of Anchor was distant from headquarters which was the reason Kate Gillenwater had selected it.

She came to Quinton and he held her tightly with a desire and hunger that he had never known before. He thought of the nights at Anchor, lying awake in his bunk, tormented by the knowledge that she was being another man's wife, and wanting her fiercely himself, so fiercely that he felt he could kill in cold blood to have her. So he would lie awake, sweating with dread and disgust and jealousy, shutting his eyes to the picture of her in Gillenwater's arms but never able to shut his mind.

Now she was his, if only briefly, fleetingly. He knew this would never suffice. She had to be his all the time, but how he could accomplish that he did not know. That other job had first call on him, the job that had no end, but he would make it have an end. He would finish it, he told himself savagely, and then he would go back to Texas and take Kate Gillenwater with him. However, he said nothing of this to her.

Afterward, they sat side by side with their backs against a boulder. He built two cigarettes and then lighted hers first. He drew thoughtfully on his, staring with a distant preoccupation through the faint tobacco smoke. He considered it strange that all at once he should be thinking of something that had nothing to do with Stony Brice or this bronze-haired woman.

She noticed his engrossment and she said, "What are you thinking about, Quinton?"

He heard her only vaguely. He did not answer her. His thoughts were heavy and troubled.

"You've got something on your mind," she said when he did not speak. "Is it about us?"

He stirred irritably because it was not about them. He took the cigarette out of his mouth, studied the smoking tip a while, then pinched it out and tossed it away.

"What is it, Quinton?" she asked again. "Can't you tell me?"

He turned his head and looked at her. She sat

there with her head thrown back a little, the bronze hair framing her features. There was tenderness in her eyes as she stared at him and it put a leap in his heart. Then he thought of that other thing and the joy went out of him.

His face was grave when he spoke. "How do you feel about all this trouble?" he asked.

He saw her brows go up. "Trouble?" she echoed.

"Between Anchor and those small ranchers."

Her eyes searched his face, probing for something. "What are you getting at?"

Irritation swept through him. "Can't you do something about it?"

"Do what?"

He hesitated, then plunged on, "Can't you talk to your husband about it?"

Her eyes narrowed. The softness went out of them. They seemed to glitter with an agate hardness. "Just what would you want me to say?" The words were spoken with a clipped and chill precision.

He made a gesture of annoyance and impatience. "Couldn't you get him to stop the war?"

"Why?"

The abrupt question pulled him up sharply with an alarming prescience. He laid a new, careful look on her. Her nostrils were flared out, her lips had thinned, the look in her eyes was as forbidding as the heights of the White Peaks.

"Don't you want to stop all this destruction and

killing?" he said, his tone rising. "Hasn't there been enough of it?"

"Bar H Bar and all the others have asked for it."

"What do you mean by that?"

"Don't you know?"

"No."

"They've squatted on Anchor land," she said stiffly. "They've rustled Anchor cattle and cut Anchor fences. Everything they've received they've asked for."

"I suppose Anchor hasn't done anything," he said acidly. "You should know—especially about some fence-cutting."

That cut her to the quick. Her chin came up, angry and resentful, pinpoints of brightness glittered in her eyes. "Tell me, Quinton," she said, her voice a throaty growl. "Whose side are you on?"

He was getting angry, too. It was all so heartless and senseless, it could have only a tragic ending, there were never any victors in a conflict as vicious and relentless as this.

"I'm on nobody's side," he said with heat. "I'm working for Anchor because I'm in love with you and not because I think Anchor is in the right. I just can't see this thing going on. There will be more destruction and killing. When will it end?"

"When Hawthorne and the others leave the White Peaks."

"Oh, Kate, Kate," he cried, getting furious, "has

the poison reached you, too? Can't you think of anything but power and money? Has living with Gillenwater made you like him? Think of the others, think of those who will have to die, not only among the small ranchers but also among those at Anchor. Won't you think of them?"

"Anchor's riders knew what they would be in for," she said, lips moving stiffly. "They're being paid for every risk they take."

He sat there appalled, staring unbelievingly at her. This was not the woman he loved, he told himself. She was not really like this. It was Gillenwater who had turned her into this.

"Kate," he cried, grabbing her arms. "Listen to me. I'm talking about human life. I've killed but only when I had no choice, but this is brutal, senseless killing. That's what I'm talking about. That's what I want you to stop. Couldn't you talk to Gillenwater about it? He won't listen to anyone else. Maybe he'll listen to you."

"What if I don't want to talk to him about it?"

He could not believe his ears. "Then you're for it?" he said hoarsely. "Then you're all for this war?"

"I'm for Anchor's rights," she declared, eyes burning. With a savage jerk she broke loose of his hold and jumped to her feet. She stood there, fists clenched, breasts heaving, glaring down at him. "If Anchor gives in now, do you think the others will stop? The fight's too far gone,

Quinton. The hate's too deep. There can be only one winner in this war, only one outfit in the White Peaks, and that outfit's going to be Anchor!"

When she was gone, Quinton was sad, not so much because of her absence although he missed her but because of the disturbing thoughts in his mind. He tried not to think of them but they kept angling in to his brain. All at once, he felt helpless and even forsaken and this sensation made him curse with impotence and vexation.

He mounted the blaze-faced black and started up a hill, no destination in mind, a vast restlessness plaguing him. He wanted to take Stony Brice and return to Texas but now he realized sinkingly that that would not be the end of it. He could not leave without Kate Gillenwater and for the first time since he had known her he had a genuine doubt that she would desert Anchor. She might no longer be in love with Clay Gillenwater but that did not mean she was tired of Anchor.

When Quinton gained the top of the hill he saw a rider below. Quinton reined in as the horseman started up the slope. It was Luke Fowler.

The old rancher was riding his buckskin. He pulled up close enough to Quinton so that the two horses nuzzled each other. Neither man exchanged a greeting. Fowler crossed his big-veined hands on the horn while his bright glance studied Quinton. The lines of Fowler's face were tired. There seemed to be new wrinkles in his brow and at the corners of his mouth.

After a long study, Fowler said, "I want to thank you for the other day, Quinton. I also want to apologize for what I said to you the first time I saw you."

"Forget it." Quinton's tone was gruff.

Fowler looked down at his hands. "I don't understand what a man like you is doing working for Anchor."

"It's a job."

"You're not happy with it, though."

"How do you know?"

Fowler's glance lifted. The eyes held an old wisdom. "There's something keeping you in the White Peaks, Quinton, and it isn't the wages Anchor is paying you."

Quinton smiled dryly. "What is it, then?"

Fowler hesitated before speaking. His tone had a hint of defiance. "I'd say it's Mrs. Gillenwater."

A sense of guilt tingled the back of Quinton's neck. If Fowler knew, then Gillenwater might also know. Then anger mounted in Quinton. He did not care who knew. He loved the bronze-haired woman and he would fight for her and kill for her, right or wrong, that was the way he felt about her. Nothing would change this feeling in him, not even death.

The look in his eyes was hard and sinister as he

stared at Luke Fowler. "Have you been spying, Fowler?"

Fowler shrugged. There was no fear in his face. "Call it what you like. I've been wondering about you ever since you pulled Clay Gillenwater off me. You're not the kind to stay on at Anchor. Then I saw you and Mrs. Gillenwater and I had my answer." His eyes clouded, they were gentle and compassionate now. "It's no good, Quinton," he said softly.

"Why do you say that?" Quinton's voice was tight. "Because she's married?"

"No," said Fowler. "I'd tell you the same thing if she had no husband."

"Why?"

Fowler spread his hands in a gesture as if trying to explain it that way. "Her and Clay are two of a kind, Quinton. Maybe they don't hit it off too well but they're alike in many ways. They're both selfish and cruel and greedy and ambitious. They're both rotten."

Wrath flared in Quinton. "I won't have you talking that way about her!" he cried, rearing up in the stirrups.

Sadness crossed the old man's face. Despite Quinton's obvious anger, Fowler's eyes still did not reflect fear. There was pity in his voice. "It's the truth, Quinton. In your own heart you know it's the truth."

Abruptly the wrath left Quinton. He sank down

in the saddle again, suddenly weary and sick at heart. He did not want to admit it but he realized that Fowler was reciting undeniable facts. It was this knowledge that made Quinton so uneasy and miserable in his love for Kate Gillenwater.

He knew very little about her, Quinton thought. She had never told him anything about herself, but then he had never told her the truth about him. As much as he loved her he still did not trust her that much, and it was this realization that made it impossible for him to get angry at Fowler. The old man meant only good.

"What do you know about her?" Quinton asked, his voice subdued. "Where is she from?"

"Nobody knows. I doubt if even Clay knows. She came to Gunsight and started dealing faro at the Palace and after a while Clay married her. That's all I can tell you—except that she's no good for you."

Irritation settled in Quinton. "Let me decide that, will you?" he said with resentment.

"I am not trying to tell you what to do, Quinton," Fowler said evenly. "If I didn't like you, I wouldn't have told you what I did. I don't care what happens to anybody on Anchor, not even Clay any more, but I don't want you to go down with them. They're bad for you, Quinton, both of the Gillenwaters. The sky is going to fall on them one of these days. I hope you'll be gone from Anchor then."

Fowler reined the buckskin around and started back down the slope, shoulders straight and head high. He disappeared into some trees without once looking back.

Quinton stared at the spot where Fowler had gone from sight for a long time. Fowler's words kept echoing in Quinton's mind—she's no good for you, she's no good for you. Quinton's fists clenched without his being aware of it. An angry denial screamed in his brain but it could not alter the truth which lay so heavy and aching in his heart.

She was no good for him but he loved her. He would love her until he died . . .

Chapter 8

The next day excitement gripped Anchor. Most of the riders were called in at noon and told to rest the remainder of the day. It became apparent what was in the offing. Anchor was going to ride that night.

Quinton was relieved when Bucky Dean was one of those left behind. The youth still had not recovered from the raid on the herd. Though he no longer talked about it, Quinton knew that Dean was still tortured by the belief that he might have killed his friend, Ben Sawtelle. Some of the melancholy had lifted from Dean but remnants of it shadowed his eyes and kept him from smiling.

They left Anchor at nightfall with Clay Gillenwater and Dalhart in the lead. As on that other occasion, Dalhart cut a gap in the fence and the cavalcade rode through but they did not split up this time. They rode under a clouded sky, working up to higher ground that lay at the base of a peak.

Quinton heard one of the men mention Flying W which was owned by Pete Corey. Quinton assumed that was their destination. He wondered what was in store for Flying W. Knowing

Gillenwater and Dalhart as he did, Quinton realized it would be nothing good.

Flying W was a series of high, steep hills mottled with trees. There was very little level ground. Quinton wondered what Gillenwater would want with land like this when he already owned the broad and rich reaches of Anchor. Then Quinton remembered the avarice and meanness that possessed some men and it made sense to him.

Flying W's buildings lay on the slant of a hill. This slope was not so steep which was the reason it had been selected when the structures were built. In the darkness the buildings were not visible to Quinton, but someone was familiar with this ground for the cavalcade was called to a halt.

Gillenwater and Dalhart held a brief, whispered consultation. Then the group split. Quinton was one of those who rode with Dalhart up a hill and then came down on Flying W from the other side. Gillenwater moved his men in from the opposite direction and Flying W was surrounded.

A dog set up a frenzied, angry barking as the riders closed in. Now that the alarm was given, Anchor's men speeded the pace of their horses, racing in at a gallop. The dog kept yelping and somewhere a door banged and then a shot rang out.

The bullet was high, obviously a warning. Dalhart fired at the gunflash without halting his horse. Some of the other riders opened up, too, and the door banged again as if someone had hurriedly taken refuge in the house.

The dog charged Anchor's riders, snarling and barking viciously. Someone swore and fired. The dog emitted a stricken, strangled growl and then was silent.

They reached a corral and Dalhart called a halt. Anchor's men dismounted and tied their horses to the corral bars. A couple of men crept along the shelter of the corral fence in the direction of a shed. Guns were roaring all about the place, streaking the night with savage tangents of orange flame.

A hail of bullets was pouring at the house and two guns in there were replying. A screaming slug chewed a chunk of wood out of a bar close to Quinton's head and he ducked down until he was flat on the ground. His .44 was in his hand but he had yet to fire a shot. His heart was sick. He cursed Gillenwater and Dalhart silently and savagely.

The two men who had gained the shed now poured some coal oil on the boards and then a match flared. At first, the fire was only a faint twinkle. Then the flames caught the oil-soaked wood and the light of the spreading fire glowed an ominous carmine. As it gained in force, the sound of its crackling became audible even above the roaring of the guns.

Someone not far from Quinton screamed in sudden pain. Quinton knew no pity, only a fierce, evil joy. He hoped it was Dalhart but then he heard the ramrod's nasal voice bawling some orders.

Across the way, some of Gillenwater's group had set the barn ablaze. As the flames of the two fires soared, a reddish, unholy light spread over the place. Quinton saw the house now, weirdly outlined in the carmine light. The two guns were still working from inside the place. That would be Pete Corey and his wife.

A man edged in close to Quinton. He turned his head and saw Dalhart there, flat on the ground beside him. The red light gave Dalhart's features a satanic cast.

"What are you saving your shells for, Quinton?" Dalhart shouted. His eyes darted to Quinton's silent gun. "Anchor's paying for the bullets, not you, so how about busting a few caps?"

"Do you need my gun that bad?" answered Quinton, rage stirring in him. "Aren't the odds big enough to suit you?"

"Damn you," cried Dalhart, twisting so that he could face Quinton. "Damn you and your smart answers." His gun started coming around, too, but then he caught sight of Quinton's .44 pointing at him. Dalhart froze, eyes wide but not with fear. They glowered with aborted fury.

An impulse to kill flared across Quinton's mind. Only the innocent died in this war, it seemed. The ones who merited death continued to live so that they might plunder and murder some more. Kill him, he told himself savagely. Kill him now before someday he kills you. But Quinton could not bring himself to fire.

A slug screeched between them, spraying their clothing with dirt. That broke the tension. Dalhart cursed and turned his head and bawled another order. Then he was going away on all fours. Quinton lay there, angry at himself and at everything, the .44 still unfired in his hand.

One of the corrals held three horses and the animals were wheeling and plunging about the enclosure in frenzied terror. From inside the barn came an equine scream that turned the back of Quinton's neck to ice. The scream went on for a long while, until the roof caved in with a roar and crash that sent a shower of sparks high in the sky.

The two guns were still going bravely in the house.

A corner of the house had just been set afire, and the man who had started it returned at a run for the shelter of the corral. He had almost gained it when a bullet caught up with him. The agony of it brought him up on his toes, head thrown back while he screamed. His arms clawed at the air like the gestures in some primitive Indian dance. Then his knees buckled and he pitched forward on his face. He kicked and writhed in pain-racked convulsions a while before he was finally and eternally still.

"Corey!" someone shouted from across the yard and Quinton recognized the voice as Clay Gillenwater's. "Come on out, Corey!"

Corey's answer was a burst of gunfire. The flames had crept up the corner of the house and now they caught on to the shingles of the roof. Cedar crackled and popped in imitation of the gun shots that still rang out.

"Come on out," Gillenwater shouted again, "or stay in there and roast. It's your choice, Corey!"

Flames began to edge along the walls of the house as the fire expanded, half the roof was ablaze, but the two guns were still blasting away defiantly. Dalhart bawled another order and the men began to creep in, working along the rim of the corral.

Quinton became aware that someone was crouched behind him. Glancing back, he saw George Marberry there, teeth flashing white in a sinister smile. The red light flicked eerily across the man's black-whiskered features. The gun in Marberry's hand was pointed almost carelessly at a spot between the ground and Quinton but Quinton knew it would take only the fraction of a second for Marberry to tip it up and fire.

"You heard Dalhart, Quinton," said Marberry, still smiling. "Get moving. I'll follow."

Quinton started along the rim of the corral,

crouched over, aware that Marberry was right behind him. Marberry's whole attention was being given to Quinton. The guns in the burning house were silent now. The flames reared ever higher.

The door opened now and Pete Corey and his wife stumbled out, arms thrown up in front of their faces and coughing rackingly. They were both unarmed and on seeing this Anchor's men came ahead with a rush. Quinton went with them, Marberry still close behind him. It was now apparent to Quinton that Marberry had been detailed to keep an eye on him.

Corey came to a halt and lifted his hands in surrender. His wife stood beside him, shoulders slumped in defeat. In the weird light of the flames Corey's face was strained and shocked as he watched all his work and dreams going up in fire and smoke.

Anchor's men formed a semi-circle as they closed in. The burning house was at Corey's back. There was no place for him to flee. He stood there with hands upraised, appearing not to care what happened to him. The utter destruction of his ranch had ripped the will right out of him.

Anchor's men were on foot but now Clay Gillenwater appeared, riding a horse. He sent the animal through the line of his men and reined it to a stop in front of Corey. Corey lowered his hands as there was no more need of keeping them raised. His surrender was abject and complete. He stood there with bowed head, staring bitterly and desolately at the ground.

Gillenwater had his rope in his hands. "You're going to be a lesson to all of them, Corey," Gillenwater shouted, his dark features sinister and evil in the flickering, crimson light. "When the others see what has happened to you, they'll get out of the White Peaks. They'll either get out or have a taste of the same."

Something in Gillenwater's voice warned Corey and his head came up but he was not quick enough. He started to throw up his hands but Gillenwater was too swift. The man had a genuine skill with a lariat and Quinton remembered Fowler's words of having taught Gillenwater to handle a rope. Gillenwater kept the noose small and he flipped it out underhanded, quick like the strike of a snake. Corey saw it coming and he tried to catch the loop with his hands but it slipped past his fingers and then dropped down over his head and in the next instant Gillenwater had pulled the noose tight bout Corey's neck. Gillenwater then made a swift dally around his saddlehorn and struck his horse with the spurs.

As the horse jumped ahead, jerking Corey off his feet, his wife cried out and started after him. She had taken only two steps when Dalhart fired. Her screaming ceased abruptly and she pitched headlong and then lay still.

Gillenwater's horse raced at a gallop past the burning barn, dragging Corey brutally along the ground. He bounced once as he caromed off a rock. Then the night shut him from sight. Only the clatter of the horse's pounding hoofs drifted back.

Quinton was angry and sick inside. Without thinking, he raised his .44 and he had it aimed at Dalhart when something poked him in the back. It was the bore of George Marberry's gun.

"It's all over, Quinton," Marberry said, his voice both amused and menacing. "There's no need for any more shooting. Why don't you holster your gun?"

Feeling sick and full of futility, Quinton put away his .44. He had to clench his teeth to keep from giving out a torrent of hot words. He could feel the muscles of his thighs trembling from the helpless wrath that raged in him.

Gillenwater returned at a gallop and reined in his horse in a cloud of dust. He was still dragging what was left of Pete Corey. Gillenwater flipped his rope off and then coiled it and hung it on his saddle. He stood up in his stirrups like a king and surveyed the destruction about him with obvious pleasure.

"I'll give them a week," he declared, making it sound like a magnanimous offer. "If they're not gone from the White Peaks by then, it will be somebody else's turn."

He nodded at Dalhart and the ramrod ordered Anchor's men to mount. As he walked to his horse, Quinton promised himself that before he left the White Peaks with Stony Brice, he would kill both Clay Gillenwater and Dalhart.

Anchor's riders were rather subdued on the way back to the ranch. A few of them chatted and joked but most of the riders were grimly silent. As hard as they were, the ruthless brutality that they had witnessed this night had left a loathsome impres-sion on them.

Quinton seethed all the way back to Anchor. He was tempted several times to pull his gun and shoot down Gillenwater and Dalhart, but then caution told him he could not get away with it. Then, too, his real job was Stony Brice. This was none of his affair. This was something he had become involved in against his will. He was staying on at Anchor because of Kate Gillenwater and because he still hoped it would provide him with the opportunity of taking Brice. He should forget about everything else, Quinton told himself, but he knew he could not ignore these brutal things that went so harshly against his nature.

Dawn had come when the cavalcade reached Anchor. Quinton was surprised to see the bronze-haired woman up this early. She was standing on the gallery, watching them ride up. She looked a little tense and apprehensive as she counted the number of those returning. The fact that her husband was one of them did not appear to reassure her. Only when she saw Quinton did she seem to relax. However she did not leave the gallery.

Quinton dismounted with the others and stripped bridle and saddle from the blaze-faced black. He turned the horse into a corral and came back to find Dalhart approaching him.

There was a portentous swagger to the ram-rod's walk. His hard glance darted to Quinton's filled shell belt. "You're kind of stingy with your cartridges, aren't you, Quinton?" Dalhart said with a sneer. "What are you saving them for?"

Quinton became aware that Clay Gillenwater had not gone to the house. Gillenwater stood to one side, watching.

The old resentment and rage stormed through Quinton. "I'm saving them for those who need killing real bad," he growled.

A sudden rush of anger colored the high points of Dalhart's cheeks. "If you were as handy with a gun as you are with smart answers, you'd be of some use to Anchor," he snarled.

"Is that why you're useful?" said Quinton with a deadly softness. "Because you can shoot down an unarmed woman?"

"Damn you, Quinton," cried Dalhart, eyes glowering. "I'm warning you. Don't rile me!"

Quinton could feel it building up in him, the long-suppressed wrath and vexation. The insufferableness of it passed through his mind like a blinding sear of light. Suddenly he wanted it over with. He wanted to kill this man that he was hating more and more. He wanted to kill him now. He had no heed for the consequences. He only wanted to kill.

Quinton set himself, all ready to grab his gun, his stare intent on Dalhart's eyes. That's where it always started, Quinton told himself. You could always see the intention there in the eyes the instant before a man went for his gun. So Quinton watched as he said:

"You'll never draw on me, Dalhart. For two reasons. I've got a gun and I'm not a woman!"

This was all that Dalhart was going to take. It was apparent in the way his mouth opened and then closed abruptly without saying a word. Dalhart was done talking. The hate and lust to kill glowed naked and feral in his eyes. One corner of his mouth twitched and Quinton, watching Dalhart's eyes, thought, here it comes.

Quinton did not know how she got there. He had been so intent on watching Dalhart that everything else had become oblivious to him. He was all set to grab at his gun handle when she was there, panting hard, halted in the line of fire between him and Dalhart.

Anger burned in Kate Gillenwater's eyes. "Stop

it, you two," she snapped. "Doesn't Anchor have enough of a fight on its hands without its men quarreling among themselves? Stop it at once."

"Step aside, Mrs. Gillenwater," growled Dalhart, glaring past her at Quinton. "Step aside."

"I won't step aside. You started this, Dalhart. If you hadn't picked on Quinton, he'd never have talked back to you. Break it up. Your job is to get along with the men, not to get into gunfights with them."

"Step aside, Mrs. Gillenwater," Dalhart said again, his tone hard and unyielding. "I'm killing the dirty son!"

"Do like she says, Dalhart!"

Clay Gillenwater said this. He spoke with a strange, veiled calmness. Dalhart sucked in his breath in a ragged, frustrated sob.

"You heard him call me," Dalhart protested. "Nobody can call me like that and get away with it."

"Let it ride, Dalhart," said Gillenwater. "Mrs. Gillenwater is right. Anchor's men should not fight one another. Anchor must pull together." Quinton thought there was a touch of sarcasm in Gillenwater's tone.

Dalhart's fists clenched. He hit down hard on his teeth until the muscles bulged along his jaw. Then he spat an obscene phrase and stalked off, stiff and taut with rage.

Quinton turned and glanced at Gillenwater.

126

The man was standing there with a thoughtful expression on his face. He fished in a pocket almost absently and finally came out with a cigar. Gillenwater's glance kept moving pensively and calculatively from his wife to Quinton and back again. That distant consideration in Gillenwater's dark eyes put the breath of a chill on the back of Quinton's neck.

He wanted to look at Kate Gillenwater but he did not dare, not with Clay Gillenwater watching the way he was. Slowly, Quinton turned and started for the bunkhouse. He was aware that Gillenwater's glance was following him.

I wonder if he finally knows, Quinton thought. I wonder if he knows now about me and Kate. Is that why he stopped Dalhart—so he can kill me like he killed Pete Corey?

Thinking thus brought a vast uneasiness to Quinton . . .

Chapter 9

The small ranchers did not retaliate for the brutal death of the Coreys until three days later. Anchor was prepared for a raid on its headquarters. Guards were posted day and night in expectation of an attack. But retaliation took a strange and feeble form.

On the third night, at a distant spot on Anchor, the fence was cut and about a hundred steers were run off. The sign of their going was very plain as though whoever had rustled the beef had been careless or indifferent or stupid. The tracks pointed up toward the vastnesses of the White Peaks.

When the theft was discovered and reported back to headquarters, Dalhart appointed six men to ride with him. Quinton was one of those selected. He thought it strange until he recalled that Dalhart had consulted with Gillenwater before issuing any orders. Quinton's selection had undoubtedly been Gillenwater's idea. Dalhart made it very plain that he did not like having Quinton along.

Clay and Kate Gillenwater were standing on the gallery of the house when Dalhart and his men left. Quinton felt his eyes being pulled toward the bronze-haired woman but he did not so much as nod his head in a gesture of farewell. Her glance passed over Quinton but it was brief and impersonal and he knew it was because of her husband standing there next to her. Gillenwater's face appeared dark with a smug pleasure as he watched the group ride away.

They reached the gap in the fence at noon and rode on through without pausing. A repair crew had followed them out from Anchor and they would close the gap in the wire. Dalhart picked up the tracks without any difficulty and he followed them at a fast pace.

The stolen cattle were being driven into rugged country. The land kept rising. The forbidding peaks loomed closer and more monstrous as Anchor's riders moved on. The air grew colder as they climbed. The men put on their jackets and buttoned them. Still they were not too comfortable.

Now the tracks entered a canyon whose walls rose high and towering on either side. A wind swept down from the heights, bringing with it the sting of ice. The horses were blowing and Dalhart called a halt to rest the animals. The men took this opportunity to dismount and stretch their legs. They built cigarettes and smoked them. There was very little conversation.

When the horses were breathing easy again, Dalhart gave the order to mount and they proceeded in their pursuit of the cattle tracks. The canyon widened until the floor of it made a long, narrow plain. They passed the crumbling remnants of a ranch house and barn which indicated that someone had tried his luck here once. But the graze was too sparse and the winters too long and rugged and so a man's dream had shattered and now lay dead and forgotten among the disintegrating buildings.

One of the riders, the gunman called Frio Bates, cried out a warning that made Anchor's men pull in their horses. Bates was staring along their backtrail. Dalhart rode his sorrel over beside Frio Bates.

"What is it, Frio?" asked Dalhart.

Bates rubbed the ridge of his lantern jaw. He had a small, wicked mouth and a tiny, fastidiously groomed mustache. He fancied himself a ladies' man although his mirror obviously told him otherwise but Bates' vanity would not admit the truth.

"I thought I saw something on that rise back there," said Bates.

"A rider?" asked Dalhart.

Bates frowned. "He was gone just as I turned my head. It could have been a rider."

"You aren't sure?"

"I'm sure I saw something." Worry creased his brow. "We're getting pretty far from Anchor, Dalhart."

"I'll decide when we've gone far enough," snapped Dalhart. "We're not going back without those cattle."

Dalhart reined the sorrel around. He flicked Quinton with a hard glance as he rode by. Dalhart kept the sorrel moving and Anchor's men resumed their tracking.

They were uneasy now. A disturbing prescience filled Quinton, too. It was nothing that he could put into words, it was something he sensed, something phantasmal but real. It put an apprehensive sensation between his shoulder blades. It was almost like the pinpoint of a knife tickling his spine.

Quinton along with the others kept throwing glances now and then along their backtrail, all but Dalhart. He rode with his eyes fixed on the cattle tracks. Now and then he raised his gaze to study the land ahead. He never once looked back.

Along toward sundown they came to a line-shack in the shadow of a white-capped peak. The land was rolling here, dotted with brush and clumps of cedar. The shack had been built in the lee of a hill. It was used only in the warmest summer months when the small ranchers grazed cattle here. It was empty now.

Dalhart called a halt. For a while he sat in his saddle with his head bowed, a slight, cold man with dark, cruel thoughts. Viciousness showed in the shape of his mouth and in the outlines of his prominent nose. He had no friends and he tried to make none. He lived only to kill.

Finally, Dalhart lifted his head and looked at the lowering sun. "We'll stop here tonight," he said.

There was a corral into which the men turned their horses. The old puncher called Pecos started a fire in the box stove and then took it upon himself to get supper. Quinton gathered up some dried cedar and carried it in beside the stove. He straightened to find Dalhart lying on a bunk, staring at him with a veiled, ominous concentration. Not wishing to tangle with the ramrod, Quinton walked outside.

The others stayed in the shack, standing around in the warmth of the stove, but Quinton preferred the chill of the outside. He wanted as little to do with Dalhart as possible. Quinton was beginning to understand why Gillenwater had sent him along with Dalhart. Perhaps Gillenwater had it figured out that the two men would tangle and that Dalhart would kill Quinton. That would serve Gillenwater's purpose very well, if his suspicions were aroused concerning his wife and Quinton.

The sun was down, the hollows were thick with shadow although the high crests were still bright and clear. Quinton lifted his glance to a ridge and there he saw the riders. On the instant a cold portentousness folded itself around Quinton's heart. Then the dread passed for he had rather expected something like this. He turned and looked at the opposite ridge and saw horsemen silhouetted there also. The line-shack was surrounded. Quinton knew now why those cattle tracks had been so plain. They had been the bait for the trap.

Quinton put his head inside the door. "Come take a look, Dalhart," he said quietly.

The mildness of his tone and the fact that he had spoken to Dalhart warned the others. Dalhart came out of the bunk quickly, spurs shrilling as he strode to the door. The others crowded after the ramrod.

Frio Bates began to curse when he spotted the riders who still showed themselves on the ridges. "I told you, Dalhart," Bates growled. "I told you I saw something but you wouldn't listen."

Dalhart turned a contemptuous look on Frio Bates. "Scared, Frio?" sneered Dalhart.

Bates flushed with anger and mortification. "You know nothing scares me, Dalhart, not even you. I'm saying you should have expected something like this after what we did to Flying W. They sucked you into a trap, Dalhart."

"If you're going to give up without a fight," Dalhart snarled, "why don't you raise your hands and walk up to them?" He laughed evilly. "I'm sure they'd give you a nice welcome."

Pecos shifted his chew from one cheek to the other. "I'd say we better figure out something to do instead of standing here chewing the rag."

Before anyone could say anything more, some of the riders on the ridges opened up with rifles. None of the bullets took effect but they sent Anchor's men scrambling hastily into the line-shack. The guns kept roaring even after the door had been slammed shut. Leaden slugs thunked into the thick log walls with sodden sounds but none penetrated. The shack was very sturdily built.

There were only two windows in the shack. Glass shattered as bullets smashed the panes. Dalhart grabbed a rifle and now with a swift, angry swipe of the barrel he completed the job of smashing the glass so that not a shard of it remained in the window. He poked the rifle over the sill and sent three quick shots up at the ridge.

Frio Bates did the same to the other window. He was joined by Blackie Kellerman and Tom Russell, two of the other riders. Another hand, named Dick McIver, joined Dalhart at his window. They kept blasting away at the ridges while the men up there answered. Only Quinton and Pecos refrained from shooting.

Dalhart turned away from the window to reload his Winchester. In the gloom his eyes sought out Quinton. A corner of Dalhart's mouth lifted in a snarl of rage.

"Still saving your shells, Quinton?" Dalhart shouted above the roar of the guns.

Quinton's eyes narrowed. He told himself to take it easy. They were in enough of a spot without him quarreling with Dalhart. "I think it would be a good idea if we all saved our shells," he answered. "You're not hitting any body and we might need our bullets real bad later on."

The logic of this dawned on Dalhart. He said nothing immediately. In the thickening gloom his thin face looked sly and thoughtful. A slug screeched through the window past his head and smashed through the smoke-pipe of the stove, twisting the tube askew. Smoke from the fire began to seep into the room.

"All right," Dalhart shouted to Bates and the others. "Hold it." As the men stopped shooting and turned to look at him puzzledly, Dalhart went on, "They've all taken cover. We won't be able to hit any of them. Let them shoot all they want. These walls will stop everything they throw at us."

Now that Anchor had ceased fire, the shooting from the ridges slackened and finally stopped entirely. A silence hung over the ridges, heavy and ominous. Quinton risked a lock out the window. Night had fallen. He could see the glittering of the stars. He stood there watching and, after a while, someone moved in next to him and glanced out. Quinton was surprised to see that it was Dalhart.

Dalhart scanned the ridge above whose top

showed faintly against the starlight. In the shadows Quinton could not read the expression on the ramrod's face but it was apparent that he was thinking hard on something.

Frio Bates said, "Well, what're we gonna do?" He sounded impatient.

Dalhart said nothing.

Bates swore again. "Dammit, we just can't stay here, here like this?"

"You got anything better to suggest?" Pecos said dryly. He had gone over and lain down on a bunk. He was old and knew the futility of rashness and impatience. He had also learned to accept misfortune as it came.

Bates swore again. "Dammit, we just can't stay here. They've got us surrounded. If we'd turned back when I'd wanted to, we'd never—"

Dalhart whirled in sudden, unrestrained fury. "Will you shut up, Frio?" he shouted. "Will you shut up before I shut you up?"

The words died uncompleted on Frio Bates' tongue. After a moment, he growled something unintelligible, then lapsed into silence. Someone up on the ridge tried a flurry of shots but when Anchor did not respond the ridge became silent again.

Blackie Kellerman said, "They can't hurt us in here. The walls are too thick. They'll keep out bullets. We're all right in here."

"Yeah," Dalhart said wryly. "What're we gonna

do for grub and water? We sure as hell can't live on air."

"Maybe we can make a run for it," Dick McIver suggested.

"What do you think of it, Quinton?" said Dalhart.

The fact that the question was directed at him surprised Quinton. Even the animosity was gone from Dalhart's tone. The query had been plain and forthright.

Quinton was still staring outside. "That's our only chance," he said. He glanced worriedly at the stars. "There's no moon which should be of some help. It would be better if we had some clouds but we can't ask for everything."

"Then you think we should make a break?" asked Dalhart.

Quinton shrugged. "We're going to have to, sooner or later."

"We'll wait a while," said Dalhart. "Maybe some clouds will come up to make it darker . . ."

The clouds, however, did not appear. If anything, the stars seemed to grow brighter, shining with a winking wickedness against the dark backdrop of the sky. Now and then shots came down from the ridges, to thunk harmlessly into the walls of the line-shack. Anchor saved its shells and did not answer. When their firing drew no reply, the men on the ridges silenced their guns.

Quinton stood at a window, looking out. He had just seen the gunflames of several shots and he knew that the men on the ridges had worked their way down in the darkness so that they were much closer to the line-shack. Dalhart and the others were stretched out on the bunks, seeking some last-minute rest before attempting the break.

Then the sight came to Quinton that laced the back of his neck with ice, and, seeing it, he remembered Flying W and it came to him that this would be nothing more than fair retribution. Even so, the realization made his entrails flinch and knot.

"Dalhart!" he called sharply.

Quinton's tone brought Dalhart to his feet swiftly. His spurs shrieked as he crossed the room with long, hasty strides. Then he was beside Quinton and the instant Dalhart spied it his breath sucked in in a sharp, startled gasp.

At first it had been only a reddish glow on a hillside but now it had mushroomed into a large, flickering, crimson pattern. The other Anchor men had also come to the window, crowding against Quinton and Dalhart. Frio Bates began cursing in a thick, angry tone. They all watched the fire on the hillside and now they saw it move.

"It's a wagon load of hay," said Blackie Kellerman, voice taut. "They've set it on fire and they're rolling it down on us."

"Well, don't just stand there," cried Dalhart. "We've got to stop them."

He snatched up his rifle and began firing at the flaming target which was gathering speed as it rolled down the hill. Bates and Kellerman also grabbed Winchesters and started blazing away. The men on the ridge opened up now. Suddenly Kellerman screamed and went hurtling back to slam up against the opposite wall. He gasped retchingly twice and then he pitched forward on his face.

The hail of bullets had driven Dalhart and Bates below the sill of the window. Bates stared at Kellerman dead on the floor and cursed in a sick, quavering tone. Dalhart shoved fresh shells into his Winchester and then he started to raise up. A slug screamed through the window and Dalhart ducked hurriedly. Another slug hit the stove and ricocheted with a banshee whine.

Quinton and McIver had gone to the opposite window but a fusillade aimed at the aperture had driven them to the floor. Tom Russell and Pecos tried opening the front door a crack but a bullet slammed into the portal and they closed it swiftly and dropped to the floor.

Russell crawled on hands and knees while bullets kept smashing into the log walls of the shack with an occasional one shrieking through the windows. Russell stopped when he was beside Dalhart.

"They've started another big fire beyond the corral," Russell announced. "It's like daylight out there."

They could see the flickering of the firelight beyond the window but they were not so interested in this one. They were all listening to the rumble of wheels coming closer. Dalhart jumped to his feet, flattening himself against the wall while he aimed the Winchester around the edge of the window, but the burning wagon was coming in on the shack from the side that had no window or door. Dalhart cursed savagely as a slug chewed wood out of the sill right next to his head.

The burning wagon hit the back of the line-shack with a sound that was like the clap of doom to the ears of the men inside. They could hear the flames hissing and crackling. It was only a matter of minutes before the fury of the fire would be transferred to the wall of the line-shack.

The guns on the ridges were abruptly stilled. The silence that now filled in was more ominous and threatening than the roar of gunfire. The cessation of the shooting indicated that the flames had caught on to the shack. There could be only one course of action for those inside. So the men on the ridges held their fire and waited.

Some of the light of the crackling flames reached inside the windows, filling the shack with a faint, eerie glow. In this flickering light

Dalhart's face looked grim and cruel. There was no fear in the man, only a savage rage and resentment over his entrapment.

He rose to his feet and the others followed suit since no more bullets were coming through the windows. Dalhart drew a deep breath that swelled his chest.

"We'll run for it in pairs," he said. "Russell and McIver, you'll go first. The rest of us will cover for you from both windows."

Russell's face looked sick. "They're waiting for us," he said. "They've got that fire by the corral. They're waiting for us to make a break for the horses. We—we'll make good targets."

"Do you want to stay in here then?" shouted Dalhart.

The crackling of the flames was growing louder. The heat was penetrating the interior of the shack, sweat stained the men's faces. The flames latched on to the shingles of the roof with a gushing rush of sound. It was like the hungry call of death to the men inside.

McIver drew his six-shooter and checked the loads in the cylinder. He was a short, stocky man with a round, reddish face. He had lived hard and now he was going to die hard. He tried to pretend that he did not care but the truth showed in the small spasmodic twitching of one corner of his mouth.

"Let's go, Tom," he said. "It's better first than

last. We'll be covered. Those greasy sack cowmen can't shoot straight anyway."

Dalhart and Bates took up positions at one window while Quinton and Pecos went to the other. Dalhart said, "All right," and began firing. Bates opened up with his Winchester and Quinton and Pecos with theirs.

McIver threw open the door and plunged out. Quinton heard Russell suck in his breath with a taut, moaning sound and then Russell was racing after McIver.

The men on the ridges opened up. McIver and Russell ran hunched over, six-shooters blazing in their fists. The firelight picked them up, outlined them harshly and mercilessly. Russell took five running strides before he was hit. He cried out and threw up his arms. He spun half around, face contorting, and then he was hit again. These bullets snuffed the life out of him and he collapsed without another sound.

McIver made it halfway to the corral. The first slug that hit him bowled him over. He rolled on the ground like a large round ball. Bullets kept kicking up dirt all around him. He came to a stop on his stomach. He hugged the ground as closely as he could and lifted his six-shooter and got off two more shots before he was hit again. This slug crashed through the top of McIver's skull and killed him instantly. He did not so much as twitch. His right arm remained extended. Only the fingers opened, allowing the six-shooter to sag to the ground.

The guns on the ridges were silent again and waiting.

Dalhart put his back against the wall of the line-shack while he reloaded his Winchester. His head was bowed as he gave all his attention to this. He seemed oblivious of the small tongues of flame that were beginning to dart in between the roof and the wall at the far end of the shack.

Quinton shoved fresh cartridges into his rifle, too. He found himself wondering if Stony Brice was out there on one of the ridges. He probably was. He had probably engineered this trap. There was no hope in Quinton, however, that he could take Brice. The way things looked right now Quinton would likely die as Russell and McIver and Kellerman had died.

Dalhart shoved the last shell home and raised his head. "Frio," he said, "you and Pecos try it now."

Frio Bates' face looked sick in the fireglow. He was a brave man when another was at the mercy of his gun. He had killed many times but death had never been as stark and imminent for him as it was at this moment.

"Why don't you try it?" he cried, sweat streaking his cheeks. "Why don't you and Quinton try it? It's easy to send someone else out there."

Dalhart's eyes narrowed in a threatening way. His voice held a low, ominous growl. "Me and Quinton will be trying it when there will be no one covering for us. You're as yellow as they come, Frio."

Bates' chin tilted in anger and indignation. Then he took another look at Dalhart's grim face and Bates' resentment fled. However, he made a display of bravado.

"I'll show you how yellow I am, Dalhart," he cried, teeth flashing in a grin although his eyes betrayed his fear. "I'm not afraid to die."

He pulled his Colt, flipped the loading gate open and studied the brass heads of the shells as he spun the cylinder. Then he looked straight ahead and said quietly, "Let's not keep them waiting all night, Frio."

Pecos went out with a lumbering run, followed by Frio Bates. Pecos was slow and Quinton did not expect him to get very far. Dalhart was blazing away at his window and Quinton kept his Winchester barking at the other. He had only gun flashes to shoot at. He had no way of knowing if he was hitting any one.

Bates, being faster, passed up Pecos, but the old man made it as far as where McIver lay dead before a bullet tagged him. Pecos stumbled and went down on one knee. He turned his head and saw McIver there and Pecos threw himself on the ground and started dragging himself to get behind

McIver. Another slug hit Pecos and ripped a moan out of him. The Colt fell from his hand but he did not try to pick up the weapon. He was intent only on getting behind McIver. Two bullets slammed into McIver but he was beyond feeling or caring any more. Then another slug got Pecos, smashing the bone of his thigh. His leg hung limp and use-less as he dragged himself ahead. He was just starting behind McIver when another bullet found Pecos' heart. He died with his good knee crooked for the last shove that would have sent him all the way behind McIver.

Bates got as far as the corral. There a bullet caught him and slammed him up against the corral bars. He bounded off them and went down on his hands and knees. He threw up his six-shooter for another shot but the hammer fell on an empty shell. He spun back and began crawling through the bars when another slug hit him. The impact shoved him headlong into the corral. Bates sprawled with his face in the dirt, but he got his hands under him and started raising himself slowly. He was halfway up when a slug smashed upward through his shoulders and emerged from the front of his neck. He threw himself sideways in agony, landing on his back with both hands pressed tight against the hole in his throat. Blood gushed through his squeezing, straining fingers. His legs thrashed, spurs scraping ragged furrows in the dirt of the corral. Then a slug smashed through Bates' brain and he was still.

The guns on the ridges grew silent again.

Dalhart leaned his Winchester carefully against the wall and then gave a look at the flames which were crackling and eating away inside the shack. Dalhart's face was luminous with sweat, soot-streaks stained his narrow, big-nosed face. He bent down and picked the six-shooter out of Blackie Kellerman's holster, then drew his own .45.

"You're next, Quinton," Dalhart said quietly.

Quinton reloaded his Winchester and transferred it to his left hand. With his right, he drew his .44 six-shooter. His heart was hammering. He had a plan but he was not too hopeful that it would work. He had studied the gun flashes on the ridges and he knew they were concentrated on the area between the line-shack and the corral. Quinton figured his only chance was not to head for the enclosure where the horses waited.

He drew a deep breath and stepped up to the door. There he paused and threw a look back at Dalhart. The ramrod stood there with two guns in his hands. His teeth showed in a sinister, challenging, mocking grin.

"Ready, Quinton?" said Dalhart. "I'll cover for you."

A chill laced the back of Quinton's neck. He recalled all the hate and venom that lay between him and Dalhart. His back would be to Anchor's ramrod. Would Dalhart resist the temptation?

It really made little difference, Quinton thought. Either way he was sure to die. He had a plan but not much faith in it. He could not have after seeing the other five perish. There was regret in Quinton, not so much because death was at hand, but because he had to die with his job in the White Peaks unfinished. He would have liked to have taken Stony Brice.

"What're you waiting for, Quinton?" asked Dalhart, still grinning. He appeared to be getting a perverted pleasure out of this.

A timber gave way at the rear of the shack and dropped in a shower of sparks. A blast of heat hit Quinton with an almost physical impact. He could feel his heart beating away with hard hammerstrokes. He thought once of Kate Gillenwater and then, clenching his teeth, he went down into a crouch and darted outside.

He half-expected a bullet to crash into his back and he was surprised when none did. The instant he was over the threshold he veered sharply to the left and ran with all the speed he possessed.

The men on the ridges were caught off guard. They had been expecting Quinton and Dalhart to break for the corral where the horses still milled and squealed with fright. By the time they recovered and shifted their sights, Quinton had reached a clump of brush and he threw himself flat alongside this as the guns opened up.

Quinton had been aware that Dalhart had

veered with him and now the ramrod landed part way on Quinton as he threw himself to the ground also. Bullets whined and snarled just above them, clip-ping bits of twigs and leaves off the bush. A gun was blazing on the slope just above them. One slug kicked dirt into Quinton's eyes. He heard Dalhart curse and then the ramrod's .45 roared and someone screamed hoarsely on the hillside.

"That's one bastard less," Dalhart growled. He began rolling over and over on the ground, making for another clump of brush at the edge of the firelight.

Quinton followed. His eyes were full of tears where the grit had stung them. As he rolled in Dalhart's wake, something burned a gash along Quinton's back. An inch lower and he'd have been as dead as Pecos and the others, he thought.

They gained the shelter of these bushes safely. This was the farthest reach of the firelight, beyond and above them the black of the night lay dark and inviting. As they passed into the shadows, they rose to a crouch and started at a run up the slope.

Bullets searched the land for them but they were no longer visible targets. Cries of consterna-tion and disappointment rose from the ridges. Dalhart whirled once and lifted his right-hand gun to throw a shot of defiance at them. Quinton grabbed the ramrod's arm.

"Do you want to let them know where we are?" he snarled.

Dalhart tensed and started to wrench away, then the logic of what Quinton had said occurred to him. He subsided without a word and followed Quinton up the slope.

The climb winded them, they were both breathing hard after a short time. They did not halt, however, until they had gained the crest of the ridge and passed over to the other side. Then they both sank to the ground, fighting for breath.

They sat there, waiting for the agony and labor to pass from their breathing. The sounds of horses moving about reached their ears. Dalhart cursed softly and replaced the spent shell in his .45.

"We need two of those horses," Quinton said softly.

Dalhart nodded. He beckoned Quinton and led the way down the slope, hugging the skirts of bushes and clumps of cedar. He stopped when they reached an outcropping of rock that jutted some ten feet into the air. They lay down on their bellies on top of this shelf and waited.

They kept hearing horses as the land was being searched for them. A rider passed just above them once and they held their breaths, fearing that he would ride upon them, but at the last instant he turned his mount back up the slope.

They had about given up hope that any one would pass by under the shelf when the ring of a shod hoof against stone told them that a horse was not far off. The sound came again, much closer, and Quinton and Dalhart got into a crouch. Their eyes strained as they studied the darkness.

Quinton laid aside his Winchester which he had carried with him. He kept the .44 clenched tight in his right fist as he waited. Dalhart had shoved his second six-shooter into his waistband. Only the .45 was in his hands.

The two riders loomed up suddenly out of the night. Their path carried them past the shelf. They rode hunched forward in their saddles, heads lowered as they searched the ground. It did not occur to them to look above.

When they passed the outcropping, Quinton and Dalhart leaped. The riders sensed them but before they could cry out or throw up their hands to defend themselves, Quinton and Dalhart were upon them. Quinton locked his left arm tight about one rider's throat, shutting off any outcry. The impetus of his leap carried the rider out of the saddle and they both hit the ground. Quinton's .44 was raised and he slammed the long barrel down along the rider's skull. He moaned briefly and went limp.

Quinton jumped to his feet and grabbed the lines as both horses started to wheel away. He was just in time. Dalhart brought his gun barrel down three times on his quarry's skull. Dalhart did not stop until the man was dead. Anchor's ramrod rose to his feet, breathing heavily from his efforts and lust to kill.

Quinton was already in the saddle. He handed the lines of the other horse down to Dalhart. There was revulsion in Quinton over Dalhart's needless killing of this man, but Quinton said nothing. They still were not out of this, he told himself. But if the day ever came, he would settle with Dalhart. One, or both of them, would never leave the White Peaks alive . . .

Chapter 10

They foiled their hunters by riding away from Anchor. They went up past timberline and here there no longer was any sign of pursuit. They made a long circle, coming in on Anchor from the west in a route reminiscent of the one Quinton had taken with Kate Gillenwater. They reached Anchor two days later.

Quinton and Dalhart spoke very little during that long ride. By mutual understanding an uneasy truce lay between them. None of the hate or dislike had dissipated. The animosity between them had just been laid away for the moment. It was inevitable that it would flare up again.

They reached Anchor an hour before sundown. Dalhart went immediately to the big house to confer with Clay Gillenwater. Quinton stripped bridle and saddle from the chestnut gelding he had ridden back and turned the animal into a corral. Coming out of the saddle shed, he threw a look up at the house and saw her standing on the gallery.

Quinton stopped. His heart quickened and a cloying ache filled his throat. He had to clench his fists and grit his teeth to keep himself from going to her. He wanted her now, he needed her very badly, but there was nothing he could do about it. He could only stand there helplessly and stare at her because she was another man's wife.

Her face looked a little drawn as if she had worried about him and this realization made Quinton both happy and sad. She stood stiffly, shoulders squared. She looked like she wanted to come to him but was forcibly restraining herself. Between them lay the barrier that was Clay Gillenwater.

Her hand lifted once like she was beckoning him, but then she caught herself and thrust the hand into a pocket of the copper-riveted Levi's she was wearing. She stared at him a moment longer, eyes full of unasked questions, then she turned abruptly and went into the house.

Quinton swore silently with helplessness and vexation. His heart was heavy and angry as he started for the bunk-shack.

Quinton was lying on his bunk, having a smoke, when Bucky Dean came in. Word had already got out among the hands about the disaster at the lineshack and concern was written all over the youth's face.

He took Quinton's hand and shook it warmly. Dean swallowed twice before he could speak. "I'm glad it was you who came back, Riley," Dean said thickly.

He sat up on the edge of the bunk and took a

narrowed look of Dean's face. Grief still haunted the depths of his eyes. "How've things been with you, Bucky?" asked Quinton.

Dean opened his mouth but then closed it without uttering a sound. His glance averted and stared into nothing. He spread his hands and shrugged. After a while, his glance came back to Quinton.

"Was it rough, Riley?" asked the youth.

Quinton's face turned grim as he remembered. "I've never been in a tougher spot," he murmured.

"I'm quitting, Riley." Dean blurted out the words. His eyes were wide, appealing for under-standing.

"You should have quit a long time ago."

"You think I'm doing the right thing?"

"You're not happy here," said Quinton. "Your heart's not in it. I can't see anything else for you to do."

"It's—it's too much for me," the youth said miserably. "First it was the herd—and Ben Sawtelle. Then Pete Corey and his wife. I wasn't in on that but still it was Anchor who did it and I'm with Anchor. I can't help feeling guilty about that, too. So I'm quitting in the morning. I'm telling Dalhart then, and afterward I'm riding on. I wanted you to be the first to know."

Quinton drew slowly and thoughtfully on his cigarette. "I wish you luck, Bucky."

Dean took a deep breath and exhaled it audibly.

"Why don't you quit, too, Riley? Why don't you ride away with me?"

I'd like to, Quinton told himself, I'd like to very much. But I've got a job here. I've got a job and a woman. I couldn't leave them if they mean my death . . .

Aloud, he said, "Sorry, Bucky. I'm staying on . . ."

In the morning, Bucky Dean packed his few belongings in a roll and then he went outside and saddled his horse. Dalhart was there, passing out the assignments of the day to Anchor's riders. Dean walked up to Dalhart, leading his horse.

"I'm quitting, Dalhart," the youth said. "I'm quitting Anchor."

Dalhart's glance narrowed. He lifted a hand and pulled at the end of his nose. He was obviously considering something even though his eyes mirrored only an opaque hardness.

Then he shrugged and said, "Go and see the boss up at the house. If it's all right with him, he'll pay you off."

"I don't want any of Anchor's money any more," the youth said harshly. "I don't want any money with blood on it!"

He swung up into the saddle and rode off. Dalhart watched him go. Dean was heading toward the mountains. It was his intention to ride through them to the other side and a new, clean world. He looked back only once, seeking

Quinton, and the youth waved and Quinton answered.

Dalhart started for the house with his spurs tinkling. A sense of uneasiness gripped Quinton. He felt alone and forsaken now that Bucky Dean had ridden away. There was no one on Anchor that he cared about any more, no one but Kate Gillenwater; and most of the time she was so distant for him that she might just as well have been living on another world.

Some of the men began discussing Dean's quitting. Two of them announced they were doing the same, for the murder of the Coreys had not sat well with several of the hands, even though they were hard, ruthless men. The two went up to the house.

It was a half hour before any one emerged and then it was only Dalhart and Clay Gillenwater. There was no sign of the other two. Gillenwater and his ramrod walked down to the corrals where Anchor's men were huddled in small groups, waiting.

Dalhart singled out several men, all of them gunslingers rather than cowpunchers, and called them to one side where he conversed with them in tones so low that the others could not hear. Quinton was one of those excluded. Gillenwater stuck his thumbs in his gunbelt and surveyed these men. The early sun glinted almost menacingly off Gillenwater's silver-plated spurs.

"Any more of you men feel like quitting Anchor?" asked Gillenwater. In the sun, the planes of his cheeks looked hard and stern. The black mustache drooping around the corners of his mouth lent his features a sinister cast.

Some of the men exchanged querying glances but none of them said anything. Gillenwater's eyes swiveled to Quinton.

"What about you, Quinton?"

"If I ever decide to quit," Quinton said quietly, "you'll hear about it."

Dalhart's group broke up now. They went into a corral and roped and saddled their horses. They also led out saddled mounts for Dalhart and Gillenwater. Dalhart came over and assigned the other men jobs about the ranch buildings. Quinton was one of these. It was plain that Dalhart did not want these men leaving the ranch headquarters today, and this knowledge struck a chill fear in Quinton.

The men rode off in pairs, scattering out, but all of them patently heading in the direction young Bucky Dean had taken. Quinton's heart was beating fast.

As soon as the riders were out of sight, Quinton hurried to the corral and roped and saddled a white-stockinged bay that had been assigned to his string. He borrowed a Winchester from one of the other men and, heedless of their warnings, rode off at a gallop.

He drove the bay hard and mercilessly. All the way he had to exercise the greatest caution. He could not afford to be seen. Nevertheless, he had to reach young Dean before any of the others did.

Where he could he stuck to the concealing shelter of pines and cedars. He topped the crests of hills and ridges with the greatest of care, then sent the bay at a drumming, headlong run down the other slope.

When the shot sounded, Quinton's belly for a moment was a mass of ice. His heart skipped a beat while anguish cried in his brain. No, no—the silent denial shrieked through him, but at the same time he realized the futility of wishfulness. Then the wrath came with a great, overwhelming rush. He had never known anger as forceful and terrible as this. Every fiber of his body trembled with its virulence.

He spurred the bay up the slope with great, lunging strides. The horse was blowing hard by the time it gained the crest but Quinton spurred it some more and it plunged down the other side. He saw them then—two men mounted on horses and the third lying prone on the ground. The prone man was Bucky Dean.

Quinton drew his .44. The sound of the bay's hoofs warned those below and they wheeled their horses. Quinton fired. His first bullet caught one of them in the chest. His horse reared at the same time and the man went sliding over the cantle of his saddle and the horse's rump to hit the ground with a hard jolt.

The other rider snapped off a shot but his horse was shying nervously and he missed. Before he could fire again, Quinton had put a slug in him, too. The man doubled up in pain. He started to go out of the saddle but then he caught the horn with his left hand and pulled himself back in the kak. He straightened up as much as he could and, grimacing with pain, lifted his gun for another shot. Quinton fired again. This slug passed through the man's heart. His horse gave a violent lunge and he pitched headlong out of the saddle. He hit the ground with his cheek first, his head twisting so grotesquely that his neck snapped.

A bullet whistled past Quinton's cheek, its breath hot and vicious so closely did it singe his skin. He whirled the bay around to face the first man who had pulled himself up to a sitting position on the ground from where he was aiming his six-shooter for another shot at Quinton. The slug that Quinton put in the fellow's chest smashed him back flat on the ground. He writhed weakly there, mouth gasping and fingers clawing at the grass as he sought to rise. Quinton spurred the bay in close, aimed at the fellow's head, and put a bullet between his eyes.

Then Quinton jumped to the ground. Bucky

Dean had his eyes open and his legs pulled in under him. As Quinton watched, Dean rose halfway up before his strength deserted him and he fell back. Quinton caught him under the shoulders and with this help Dean rose to his feet but he could not stand alone. He was a dead weight clinging to Quinton.

The youth was badly hurt, Quinton saw. However, the shooting was bound to attract the other Anchor men. He and Dean had to get away from here. It would be certain death for both of them if they remained here.

Quinton boosted Dean on his horse. It was obvious that the youth could not stay in the saddle and so Quinton hastily tied the youth in his kak with his lariat. Then, mounting his bay, Quinton grabbed the reins of Dean's horse, leading the animal as they galloped away.

Pursuit lasted until darkness made tracking impossible. Only then did Quinton stop. The horses were badly fagged.

Bucky Dean was unconscious in the saddle. The ropes alone held him in the kak. He hung against the ropes as limp and indifferent as if death were already upon him. Looking at the boy's face in the shadows, Quinton realized it was not far off.

Quinton untied the ropes and eased the youth to the ground. Quinton did not dare build a fire for fear that the light might attract Anchor's men should some of them be prowling in the night. He wrapped Dean in the saddle blankets and then sat down on the cold earth beside the youth.

Quinton built a cigarette and lighted it. He was tired but sleep would not come. He sat and smoked and watched the steely, distant glittering of the stars. A cold wind moaned down off the mountains but Quinton had selected a spot against a bank of pines which broke the wind, but nevertheless the cold was very pronounced.

Bucky Dean was muttering in delirium. The words were deep and garbled in his throat so that Quinton could not make any of them out. Now and then the youth stirred restlessly, throwing off the blankets, and Quinton would patiently rearrange them. Once a violent chill struck the youth and his teeth chattered with an audible sound. But the ague passed and Dean was quiet again, except for his delirious mumbling.

At last, Quinton stretched out and propped his head on the cold leather of his saddle. He did it mostly to ease his cramped muscles, he did not expect to sleep. But after a while he dropped off. He did not know how long he slept. A loud shout awakened him.

Quinton sat up abruptly, his hand grabbing the handle of the .44 at his side. The cry was repeated and Quinton turned his head and saw Bucky Dean sitting upright. The boy cried out once more—something that sounded like "Ben! Ben!"—then he dropped back and lay breathing heavily.

Quinton called the youth's name. He called it a second time but Dean did not answer. He was still unconscious. He rolled restlessly as Quinton sought to cover him with the blankets again. He kept chattering unintelligibly about something.

Some time later his mumbling stopped. His breathing grew very deep and heavy and labored. There were times when it seemed to have stopped and just when Quinton was sure it had it would resume once more, but slower, each breath spaced farther apart.

An hour before dawn Bucky Dean died.

Chapter 11

In the first dim light of that morning, Quinton carried the dead body of Bucky Dean to a small depression and then covered it with stones. Afterwards, self-consciously even though he was alone, he removed his hat and tried to remember a few snatches of prayer.

He turned Dean's horse loose and then saddled the white-stockinged bay and rode off without another look at Bucky Dean's grave. Quinton felt it was not necessary. He would remember it as long as he lived.

He rode warily, studying his backtrail often. He expected pursuit to continue, even after Dean's grave was found. This was Clay Gillenwater's way of crushing the incipient rebellion among his riders. Had Dean been allowed to quit, others would have followed his example. Gillenwater was out to demonstrate that no one could quit Anchor. Now that Quinton had aligned himself against Anchor, he would have to die, too.

Quinton had not eaten in twenty-four hours. He took the chance and killed a jackrabbit. He rode into a thick grove of pines and built a small fire, hoping the smoke would not rise too high and thick. He cooked the rabbit without salt and ate it ravenously. He was wondering all the while if the shot and the thin smoke of his fire had been picked up by Anchor's men.

He rode to a high point of ground and studied the land below carefully. Nothing stirred on the mountainside. Only the slopes and the trees, an immense inanimateness, appeared in his gaze. He rode on.

His mind dwelt on many things, all of them troubling him. He could not help but think that his life had taken a strange and complicated quirk since he had come to the White Peaks. Before then, life had been quite simple and direct. He had left the Trinity down in Texas on the trail of a killer. He had expected it to be a long trail but he had been confident it would have an ending. At its end he would take the killer and return with him to Trinity.

The trail had come to an end that day in Gunsight. But the killer was still unapprehended, and since then Quinton had fallen in love with a bronze-haired woman who was another man's wife. He had also earned the enmity of the small ranchers of the White Peaks and now he had fallen out with Anchor and was being hunted by Anchor's riders. An odd, bitter smile curved his mouth as he thought on this. From the hunter he had turned into the hunted.

Disgust and bitterness welled up in him. He told himself he should have taken Stony Brice that day in Gunsight. He should have come right out and told Wes Hawthorne and the others the truth. They might not have sided with Brice then, in which case Quinton's job would have been done. He could then have ridden back to the Trinity before becoming involved in all this hate and greed and viciousness that were rampant in this range.

It was the middle of the morning before Quinton sighted the riders. He reined in the bay on a high vantage point to rest the animal and also to scan his backtrail. He built a smoke and had just popped it into his mouth when he spied the three riders far below. The cigarette stayed unlit in Quinton's mouth.

He could hear his heart beating at a quickened pace. A strange, even frightening excitement gripped him. His eyes narrowed as he sought to identify the riders below. That they belonged to Anchor Quinton had no doubt. However, he wanted two of them to be Clay Gillenwater and Dalhart.

Quinton reined the bay over behind the cover of a cedar and peered around the edge of the tree. The riders below rode with bowed heads as they read the tracks laid down by Quinton's bay. Quinton waited until he was pretty sure one of the three was Dalhart. The fact that Gillenwater was not one of them provided Quinton with a distinct disappointment. However, he was viciously glad that Dalhart was one of them.

Quinton touched the bay with his spurs and rode off at a lope. This was rugged country here. The slopes were steep, precipitous ramparts reared here and there, and looming high and awesome above all else were the white-capped summits of the mountains. Timber dotted the hillsides and Quinton stuck to the shelter of the trees. The fact that the tracks of his passing were plain did not disturb him. He wanted it this way. He wanted to be trailed. He would stop when the lay of the land suited him. Since he would be giving away odds of three to one, he felt he was not asking too much for himself.

It was noon when he came out into the open on a high ledge. Stopping the bay, he built another cigarette and tried not to heed the pangs of hunger that assailed him. He watched with narrowed, studious eyes until finally the three riders emerged from a stand of pine below him. Though he was in plain view, Quinton stayed where he was.

The three below were not aware of him at first. They rode on a short distance, all the while reading his tracks on the land. Then one of them happened to glance up and when he saw Quinton up above this one pulled in his horse sharply and raised a hand, halting his companions. It was Dalhart.

A while they were frozen like that, an immobile, startled tableau, then Dalhart reached for the butt of the Winchester under his leg. The sun was winking off the barrel when Quinton wheeled the bay. He was gone from sight behind a cedar when the slug came screaming up at the heights.

Quinton lifted the bay into a hard run. The bay's hoofs made a sharp, drumming crescendo as it galloped across an expanse of hard ground. There was dense timber ahead in this canyon and Quinton sent the bay streaking for the trees.

A gun roared faintly behind him but the range was too long. He did not bother to look back. He knew they would come. They would persist with a dogged, brutal tenacity until either he or they were dead. At this moment, he was almost indifferent to the thought of dying. He did not mind, if he could take them with him. He felt that much was owed to the memory of Bucky Dean.

The bay raced into the trees and Quinton kept it going until it had sped up a slope. The timber was very thick here. The trees grew so close together in places that the sunlight could not penetrate. In these spots of perpetual shadow there were still scattered patches of dirty, crusted snow.

Quinton halted the bay and dismounted. He believed that on foot he would have his best chance. He could take better advantage of the cover of trees and convolutions of the land than if he were in the saddle. He tied the bay to a cedar and then he removed his spurs and hung them on the horn. Taking his Winchester, he went off at a fast walk through the timber.

He climbed until the ground leveled off for a short way. He deliberately crossed a patch of snow, high heeled boots making deep imprints, and when he was beyond it a small distance, he made a circle and doubled back. He came to a small depression in the ground and he lay down on this. The trees here made long avenues, clear of underbrush. He could see alternate patterns of sunlight and shadow as he stared across at the patch of snow which he had crossed.

Somewhere in the timber a jay called, raucous and loud. After a while it was still and a solemn silence settled over the timber. Quinton lay in his hole, only his head showing above the level of the ground. The air was cool but still sweat came crawling out on his brow. He could also feel it running down his sides beneath his clothing. His chest pressed against the earth and his heart drummed against this as against a sounding-board.

Quinton lay there quietly, waiting. Once he thought he heard a twig snap and this brought him sharply alert, but though his ears strained he could not catch a repetition of the sound. He lay there, tense, his hands sweating where they gripped the Winchester. The only thing he heard was the vast silence of the mountain.

The thought came to him that if he were killed Stony Brice would never be made to account for those killings on the Trinity. It was not the dying that worried Quinton. It was the knowledge that if he were killed now he would have failed his job.

When the sound came again there was no doubt as to its reality. Quinton propped the Winchester against his shoulder and squinted down the long barrel at the patch of snow. He waited with his heart lodged in his throat and after what seemed to be an interminable stretch of time the man came into view.

He moved slowly and cautiously, alternately studying Quinton's tracks and the forest. There was a rifle in the man's hands and he carried it out in front of him in such a position that he could whip it instantly to his shoulder and snap off a shot.

He started across the snow and when he was in the exact center of the patch Quinton fired. The report of the Winchester was loud and sharp in the silence of the timber. The echoes went rolling through the canyon with a lingering reluctance.

The man jerked spasmodically and dropped abruptly on both knees. His chin fell and it looked like he was going to pitch forward on his face but then he caught himself. His shoulders squared and his head started to lift and the rifle began coming up in his hands. Quinton was all set to fire again when the man suddenly slumped and toppled over. He lay with his face shoved into the snow, his blood forming a bright, scarlet pool among the whiteness.

A bullet smashed into the ground in front of Quinton's face, kicking dirt into his eyes. He huddled down as low as he could in the hollow while tears washed the grit out of his sight. Slugs snarled and whined above him. One hit a nearby tree with a sickening crunch.

Quinton's eyes cleared. He replaced the spent shell in his Winchester. When a lull came in the firing, he crawled out of his hole and then, springing to a crouch, went off at a run through the trees. He could not afford to remain in the hollow because there were two of them left and while one of them pinned him down the other could circle and come in on Quinton from behind. So he ran with bullets whistling past him. They kept smashing into the trees all about him but none tagged him. After a while they ceased.

He came to a slope and climbed this, breath hot and stifling in his throat. He was bathed in sweat by the time the slant of the hill eased. The timber ended abruptly and Quinton saw a small patch of open ground ahead. The land here was littered with boulders and clumps of brush and farther on the timber began again.

Quinton estimated he had a good enough lead on his pursuers who were also on foot. He raced across the open patch, darting from stone to stone. Grabbing the branches of a bush, he hauled himself up on a tiny shelf which gave him a commanding view of the timber he had just left.

Quinton lay on his belly, watching the bank of the trees. The sun beat directly down on his back, filling him with a pleasant warmth. Gradually, his breathing slowed, his lungs did not want to burst any more. He wiped sweat out of his eyes with the back of a hand and waited.

The first glimpse Quinton got was just a hint of movement, a tiny stirring at the edge of the timber. His eyes narrowed as he strained to see. The movement came again, more deliberate this time, and a man's head showed and then his shoulders. Quinton took a bead and fired.

The sun glinting off the barrel of the Winchester warned the man at the edge of the trees. He started to duck back even as Quinton squeezed the trigger. As the gun recoiled against his shoulder, Quinton knew he had missed. He levered another shell into the breech and went on watching the timber.

Suddenly, a gun began to bark down in the trees, throwing a stream of bullets at Quinton. Slugs wailed shrilly as they ricocheted off stone. He was forced to draw back from the edge of the shelf and still the bullets kept coming. They continued until the man in the timber had emptied his rifle.

When the shooting ceased, Quinton edged

forward and chanced a quick look but he could see nothing in the timber. It had sounded like one gun down there and Quinton drew back again and thought on it. The rifle opened up again but there were only two shots this time, a tentative probing at Quinton's position. The two had split up, Quinton was sure. They were trying to get him in a crossfire. He thought a little more on it and then he quit the shelf.

He had to show himself as he darted behind a bush and a bullet singed the air next to the skin of his neck. Then he was throwing himself to the ground as several slugs shrieked through the brush, clipping twigs and leaves in a whining fury. Quinton crawled on his belly until he was behind a stone.

There was more timber ahead although the trees were not so dense here and Quinton headed for this. Another slug whistled past above his head as he revealed himself once. Then he was in the trees, moving cautiously along, a sense of fore-boding, of a great and hidden menace lacing the back of his neck.

He came to a windfall and he dropped flat behind this to catch his breath. He was thinking that they would have to come to him. They wanted him, they were the hunters and he was the hunted, but the advantage lay with him because he could wait. But they were two, he thought worriedly, and now they had split up and he could never be sure when one of them would come up on his back while he was concentrating his attention to the front. A feeling of misgiving settled over him.

The gloom here in the trees depressed him. He began to get jumpy. Every now and then the sensation came to him that hidden eyes were glaring at his back and he would turn his head sharply and scan the forest back there until his eyes ached and always there was nothing to see. He edged along the windfall on his belly until he lay in a narrow space between the fallen timber and the bole of a pine. He was concealed very well here, he thought, and so he waited.

He waited until an eternity ended, it seemed, and another one began. He stopped sweating and the cold started to penetrate his clothes. Once a chill turned his spine to ice. His hands grew numb and he kept shoving them through the flap of his jacket under his shirt to warm them next to his skin. He started to doze and abruptly came awake with a sharp intuition of peril.

He gripped the Winchester tightly and eared back the hammer. Someone was moving along the windfall on the other side. Quinton could ear the soft scrape of cloth against the timber and against the ground. Once he caught the sound of a muted breath and his grip on the Winchester tightened still more while sweat popped out on his brow.

Suddenly, not five feet from Quinton, a head

came over the top of the windfall. The shoulders appeared also and then the man was staring directly at Quinton. Horror and the imminence of the inevitable distended the fellow's eyes and contorted his features. His mouth gaped wide as he prepared to emit a shout of startlement and fear but no sound emerged for Quinton fired.

The slug slammed into the man's face and crashed through his brain, snuffing out his life instantly. He pitched forward over the windfall with his arms dangling down one side and his lax legs down the other. He jerked convulsively once and then was still.

The muscles were quivering with reaction in Quinton's belly as he levered another cartridge into the breech and then replaced the spent shells. This left only Dalhart, he was thinking, but this place was not good any more. The shot and the dead man hanging over the windfall gave his hiding-place away.

He edged up until he was just barely peering over the top of the windfall. His hat he had pushed off his head so that it hung down his back from the chin thongs. A long while he studied the serene, impenetrable face of the forest but there was nothing he could see. This, however, was not necessarily reassuring and his flesh crawled as he rose behind the fallen timber and started through the trees.

Once he thought a twig snapped behind him

and he whirled, Winchester thrust out in front of him, teeth bared in a snarl. His flesh flinched in expectation of the impact of a bullet but none came. He backed up until his back was against the trunk of a tall pine and he stayed a while like that, squinting eyes searching the trees. Only the bland face of the forest stared back at him.

He started on again. Every once in a while he had to get himself in hand and slow down for his steps would have quickened as the first stirrings of panic began in him. The gloom was ominous and depressing. The mysterious depths of the timber seemed alive with unseen dangers. Sweat channeled down the beard stubble on his cheeks.

Finally sunlight showed again ahead as he neared another clearing. He stayed in the fringe of the timber, however, as he circled the open ground, eyes studying the rim of the trees across from him. He glanced up once and from the position of the sun he reckoned it was late afternoon. He had not thought so much time had elapsed.

He came to a tiny creek and dropped on his belly and drank avidly. He rose with water dripping from his chin, apprehensive eyes studying the land all around. Then he started walking along the bank of the creek.

The land rose abruptly and now the creek was replaced by a silvery cascade that plunged from a ledge fifty feet up. Quinton halted in the cover of two cedars growing close together and pondered the country above. After a short hesitation, he started to climb.

At one time, for half a minute, he was starkly in the open as he sought to pull himself up over the naked edge of a shelf. His ears strained for the angry shriek of a bullet, ice formed in the pit of his stomach, then he was over the rim, breathing hoarsely as he lay flat on the ground. After a moment, he resumed his climb, but here there were boulders and clumps of brush to conceal his progress.

When he gained the ledge, he stretched out on his back for a little while. He shut his eyes while he caught his breath. He tried to rest but knew this was not the occasion for it. As long as death waited for him in this canyon he could not rest.

Quinton rolled over on his stomach and pulled himself ahead enough so that he could peer over the edge of the small cliff. The ground was fairly open for quite a way below and he watched it a long time before he spotted anything.

It was a blur of movement among some brush and he had to wait for its repetition before he was positive about it. Then he saw Dalhart. It was only for a moment, however. Dalhart showed briefly, stealing along crouched over, and Quinton whipped the Winchester to his shoulder and drew a bead but then Dalhart passed from sight behind an outcropping of rock before Quinton could fire. The way Dalhart was taking carried him away from the ledge.

Quinton considered this only a moment. Then he started scrambling down the cliff again. He took the chance that Dalhart might turn back and catch him helpless on the way down, but Quinton gambled that Dalhart had no idea Quinton was behind him.

He picked up Dalhart's tracks easily. Quinton hurried as much as he could but he had to exercise caution for Dalhart would be studying his back-trail now and then. The tracks led up a slope, always skirting trees and bushes, and down the other side they veered in the direction of the creek again. Quinton's heart was beating hard as he entered a copse of cedar.

At the other side of the trees, he could hear the faint gurgling of the creek. Quinton edged along, careful not to make any noise, the Winchester held ready at his hip. He came to the other edge of the cedars and from there he saw Dalhart.

Anchor's ramrod was just rising from a drink of the water. Quinton could have dropped him there but he wanted Dalhart to see who it was.

"Dalhart," he called softly, cheek against the cool butt of the Winchester while his right eye looked down the long barrel at Dalhart.

Dalhart whirled with the alertness and swiftness of a striking puma. His rifle blared but the sound was the barest echo to the roar of

Quinton's Winchester. Dalhart cried out in pain and the rifle fell from his hands. His knees started to sag but then he gathered some strength and braced himself on wide-spread feet. His right hand made a blinding pass at his .45 and the barrel of the six-shooter glinted in the sun as it rose.

Quinton fired. This slug slammed Dalhart back, staggering, until he was standing ankle-deep in the creek. His face strained with agony, his eyes bulged. He still hung on to his .45, however, and as Quinton fired again Dalhart managed to snap off a shot that whipped the hat from Quinton's head. This slug turned Dalhart half around and he looked like he was going to fall sprawling in the water, but he completed the pirouette and reeled out on the shore again. His .45 started to rise once more.

Quinton fired a fourth time. The six-shooter dropped from Dalhart's hand as pain doubled him up. He made a half-circle on shuddering legs and then pitched forward. His body lay on dry land but his face was thrust into the water.

Chapter 12

Quinton picked up his bay and then he rode around until he found where Anchor's mounts had been tied. He unsaddled the horses and turned them loose. When they returned to Anchor, it would be apparent what had happened to Dalhart and the other two.

Quinton found some grub in Dalhart's saddlebags. It looked as though Anchor's ramrod had been prepared for a long hunt. As Quinton hungrily bolted the food down, he thought of this and smiled grimly.

By this time the sun had gone down. Shadows were gathering over the land. Quinton found a spot at the foot of a rocky rampart and made camp. There were pines growing all around and these and the rearing palisade sheltered him from the cold wind moaning off the icy peaks.

He was cold and tired and beyond caring about anything any more. He forgot about caution and danger and the lurking of death. In the last dimness of the day he gathered some dried wood and built a fire. It occurred to him that the trees and the rampart would shield the light of the flames but at this moment this was not an important consideration to him. All he wanted was some warmth and sleep.

He had retained the saddle blankets from Anchor's horses and now he wrapped himself in these, indifferent to their stench. The fire was crackling loudly. Almost the instant Quinton touched the ground he dropped off.

He had strange, garbled dreams. In these he was hunted and trapped and killed by a sad-eyed youth and a bronze-haired woman while Dalhart and Clay Gillenwater watched with gloating enjoyment. Once Quinton came violently awake, jerking upright in his blankets, ears straining for some alien, menacing sound in the night. His heart was beating fast. He reached down and drew his .44 from the holster which he had placed beside his head. A long while he was like this before reason assured him that this was just a fanciful product of his troubled dreams.

The fire was just glowing embers. He poked these up and added wood. By the time the flames were crackling again, Quinton was asleep.

He slept past dawn. When he awoke, the high peaks were bright with sunlight although the low country was still covered with light shadow. The fire was a long time dead and he did not bother to start it again. He chewed on some cold jerky and drank some water. Then he saddled the bay and rode away.

He did not travel much this day. The bay

moved slowly and aimlessly without much direction from Quinton. By the middle of the morning he had come to an open spot where the sun was warm. He dismounted and lay down on his back and soaked in the heat. He dozed a while and awoke refreshed, but he still did not know where he was going.

Now and then he stopped on high ground to study the country. This day, however, he saw no riders. He was the only living thing in this part of the White Peaks, it seemed, except for some buzzards he saw now and then, drifting down to where Dalhart and the others lay dead. Quinton had not bothered to bury them. They would not have done it for him.

By noon he had ridden out of the canyon and suddenly he wanted to get away as far as he could from it. He lifted the bay into a trot and rode until the sun was low in the west.

This night he camped beside a small mountain spring. Again he built a fire and sat a long time staring into the flames. He wanted to get out of the White Peaks. He wanted to finish his interminable job in the worst way but he still did not know how to go about it. This realization made him curse vexedly.

If he did manage to take Stony Brice, the small ranchers would be without their only leader experienced in violence and range warfare. Although Dalhart was dead, Anchor still had

181

Clay Gillenwater and George Marberry and some others. The small ranchers needed Brice's leadership very badly. Without him, they were done. Quinton's teeth clenched and he swore bitterly. He should never have become involved in this war, he told himself, but if he had it to do over again he knew he would do it the same —all because of a bronze-haired woman.

Finally, he rolled himself in his blankets and went to sleep.

He awoke in an ugly mood. He felt mean and spiteful because he still had not reached a decision. He was tired of being forever thwarted. What made the whole matter so insufferable was that it appeared it would never have an ending.

He rode the mountains with eyes slitted truculently, spoiling for trouble. He had not shaved since leaving Anchor and a black beard stubble covered his cheeks and rimmed his mouth and darkened the front of his neck, all of this giving his face a sinister, forbidding appearance.

With the sun at high noon he came out on a ledge which he remembered as the same one on which he had stopped with Kate Gillenwater that first day he had come to the White Peaks. He stopped the bay and hooked his right knee around the saddlehorn. He took out the makin's and built a cigarette.

He smoked mechanically, brooding glance

studying the land below. When the smoke was a butt, he rubbed it out on the horn and dropped it to the ground. He put his foot back in the stirrup and was about to rein the bay around when he spied a movement below.

His heart quickened and excitement surged in him. The way he felt right now he welcomed more trouble and violence. He welcomed more dying, even if it would be his own.

The movement came again and now a rider emerged from a stand of trees. Quinton's heart froze and on the moment he could not believe his eyes. Then a swift joy raced through him.

The rider below was Kate Gillenwater.

Her head lifted and she saw him up on the ledge. She waved an arm in recognition and spurred her palomino into a run. He sat there rather tense in the saddle, narrowed eyes scanning all the country below. Inside he was a mixture of emotions. There was happiness in him, and longing, and under these a strong current of dark suspicion.

However, no other riders appeared. After a while, he told himself angrily that he was being too jumpy. The events of the past few days and the feeling of loneliness and frustration had him all on edge. Still this argument did not allay the uneasiness in him.

He reined the bay away from the rim of the ledge and rode him over to the edge of some trees. Here Quinton dismounted. He was out of sight of anyone below—if there was anyone down there. He grew angry at himself again for thinking like this, but it seemed he could not help it.

It took her a while to reach the ledge. Quinton could hear the palomino blowing before it appeared. He stood there with his feet spread apart, the flaps of his jacket open, thumbs hooked in his cartridge belt, shoulders thrust forward, a dark, sullen, troubled man.

She halted the palomino and jumped to the ground in a great hurry. Then she stopped, staring at him with her face strained with concern. A hand rose to rest against her mouth as if stifling a cry but no sound had come from her. She stood there, wide eyes looking half fearfully at him, afraid of what they might see. Below the wide brim of her hat the ends of her bronze hair draped about her shoulders.

She took a step ahead, hesitant, uncertain, obviously set back by his sinister appearance. "Quinton?" she said, her voice atremble, sounding much like a frightened little girl. "Are you all right, Quinton?"

He said nothing. He stared at her.

She drew in her breath in a ragged sob. "Did they hurt you, Quinton?"

He did not speak now either, but it was because his throat was too full. He shook his head.

"Oh, Quinton, Quinton," she cried, running to him.

He gathered her in his arms and put his mouth down hard on hers. He could feel her shuddering in his embrace. Some of her tears moistened the beard stubble on his face. He held her until she moaned with pain and then squeezed harder. The ugliness was roiling him. He wanted her hurt in compensation for the torment and misery he had undergone. She was no good for him, he loved her but it was a futile, hopeless love, a love that could never know a normal, untroubled consummation. The one woman he had ever loved he could not have in an honest and sweet way. It had to be sneaking and sordid, in a manner which at times filled him with revulsion, but which he could not resist. So he did not care that he was hurting her. He was rough and almost brutal with impatience and anger. She cried out loudly but he paid no heed. This was the love that would never bring him any serenity or gratification. It could very possibly bring him his death.

Afterward, he felt shamed and a little remorseful, but it had all been so overwhelming that he had been swept away by it. It did not, however, change the conviction in his mind. The sense of doom and futility would not leave him. The anger and hunger were gone for now, replaced by a sweet, poignant sadness.

He had averted his face and now he felt her

fingers touch his whiskered cheek gently and then, tenderly insistent, turn his head until he was looking at her. This close he could see the tiny gold specks in her green eyes.

"I was so worried, Quinton," she said, lips trembling ever so slightly. "I was so afraid for you, even when they didn't return. I just had to come to see how you were."

He still could not speak to her. He took her hand and kissed the palm.

Her eyes were searching his face. "Their horses came back to Anchor alone. Where—where are they, Quinton?"

He nodded his head in the direction of the canyon.

"Are they—dead?"

He inclined his head.

"All three of them? Dalhart, too?"

"It was them or me, Kate."

"Oh, I'm glad they didn't hurt you," she said fervently. Her arms embraced him. He felt her shudder again. "You don't know the hell I went through, Quinton. I didn't know until it was too late to warn you. All I could do was wait. Have you ever waited like that, Quinton?"

He thought of the long, drawn-out stalking duel in the canyon. Remembering it put the feel of ice against his spine. He knew he would not forget it for a long time, perhaps never. However, he said nothing.

When he did not speak, she went on, "I almost died from fear and worry, Quinton. Then the horses came back, all three of them without their saddles. Still I thought you might be hurt." Her voice broke. "You might be dying all alone up here." She dug her face against his breast, her voice was muffled. "I died a thousand deaths, Quinton. That's why I came up here. Even if it meant finding you hurt or even dead. I just had to know, my darling."

She was crying softly now. He stroked her hair while the sadness deepened in him. He was thinking that they could have had a good life together had he met her somewhere other than in the White Peaks and before she was another man's wife.

After a while her sobs ceased. She rubbed her eyes with her knuckles and then lifted her head, showing him a wan smile. Something in it made his eyes sting and he looked away.

"Would you come back to Anchor, Quinton?" she asked.

He stiffened instinctively. A rush of suspicion started the wrath anew in his brain, but then he forced the anger from him.

"That's a strange question, Kate," he said slowly. "You know what I've done. Dalhart is dead by my hand and four other Anchor riders. Anchor is the last place I'd go to."

"Would you come back for me?"

He put his glance on her with a studied deliberateness, eyes crinkling. He did not answer right away. "What do you mean by that?"

"Would you take Dalhart's job?"

He averted his face again. "I would say that's the last job on earth I could get."

"But it isn't," she cried earnestly. "You can have it if you'll only come back to Anchor."

His gaze shifted back to her. A faint skepticism clouded the depths of his eyes, the planes of his cheeks were gaunt and wary. "What about—your husband?"

"I've already talked to him," she said. Her fists clenched about the flaps of his jacket with an urgent eagerness. "Oh, he didn't like the idea, Quinton, and I didn't tell it all to him, but I pointed out that Dalhart was dead and Slim Sunderland and Frio Bates. He wants to make George Marberry ramrod but Marberry doesn't have enough brains for the job. I told Clay you were the best man for it. You're hard and smart and the men will respect you and obey you. Anchor couldn't have a better ramrod."

"You know I can't go along with what Anchor's doing."

"That's just it," she cried. "Don't you see, Quinton? If you were foreman of Anchor, you could do something about it, couldn't you?"

He stared at her long and searchingly. "That's

quite a change from what you told me once, isn't it, Kate?"

Her eyes faltered and then her head dropped until it rested against her breast. A small shudder shook her. "I—I didn't think it was going to be like this. I can't stand all this senseless killing and destruction. If you were ramrod of Anchor, you'd have a chance to stop it."

"I'd still be taking orders from your husband."

She lifted her head and looked up at him. A hand rose and caressed his cheek. "You asked me once to talk to him, didn't you? Would you come back to Anchor, Quinton, if I promised you I would do my best to get Clay to end this war?"

This was a question that needed no answering. The reply was etched in his heart. He had not wanted to leave the White Peaks, he could not leave them as long as his job was undone. Now he could see an end to the long, frustrating hunt. If peace should come to the White Peaks, he could reveal his true identity and purpose and take Stony Brice and return to the Trinity. But something else was troubling Quinton's mind.

His heart wrenched as he looked at her. "What about me and you, Kate?"

"We'll be near each other."

"That's not enough for me."

She colored ever so slightly. "We'll find times to be together."

"I don't want it that way," he said fiercely, his

tone harsh. "I want you to be mine always, not just now and then. I want to call you my own open and proud, I don't want to keep sneaking around about it." His heart was hammering, there was a surge in his blood. "Will you go away with me, Kate? When the war is over, will you come away with me?"

She lowered her head and pressed her face against his shirt. Her voice came small and muffled. "Do you think it would work out?"

Hope rushed through him. "Why shouldn't it?" he said, a thickness suddenly filling his throat, making it hard and painful for him to speak. "We could go someplace where we're not known. It's a big country, Kate, and we could start over, just the two of us. I want you, Kate. You don't know how much I want you."

Her face stayed against his chest as she would not look at him. "Will you come back to Anchor then?"

Kate suggested that they try a more direct return to Anchor, by way of Flying W which was abandoned now that the Coreys were dead. Quinton agreed and they rode at an easy trot across the land.

They rode through a grove of pines and started down the grassy slope of a ridge. They had reached the bottom when some intuition prompted Quinton to look up and there on the slopes on either side of him he saw the riders.

Wrath, swift and ugly and fierce, rushed through Quinton. He spotted Clay Gillenwater mounted on a big white stallion. Gillenwater's arm raised in a signal.

Kate cried out, not very loudly, and started to plunge the spurs into her palomino's flanks. Quinton, however, had reacted quicker. A sharp, hard jab of his rowels jumped the bay ahead, next to the palomino. Reaching out swiftly, he grabbed the bronze-haired woman about the waist. She cried out in alarm and then he was jerking her roughly out of her saddle and carrying her across in front of his own. With his left hand he held her now as the palomino shied away. Quinton's right hand pulled his .44. He shoved the big bore of the weapon against the small of Kate Gillenwater's back.

Sunlight was glinting off the guns in the hands of Anchor's riders. They pulled up, however, when they saw what Quinton had done. Clay Gillenwater's stallion milled nervously, as though mirroring his master's uncertainty.

Quinton spurred the bay up the slope straight at Gillenwater. Kate turned her head and threw a fearful, distraught look at Quinton. Her mouth worked as though she were trying to speak but no words emerged. She stayed quietly in front of him, however, struggling not at all against his tight, angry grip about her waist.

Behind him, Quinton was aware that the riders had come down the opposite slope and were following him up this one but he did not care. He was too full of wrath and bitterness to care about anything. His eyes were irate slits and his lips parted a little, showing his clenched teeth. A trickle of sweat crawled hesitantly down through the beard stubble on either cheek.

Above him, Anchor's men waited. Clay Gillenwater's white stallion kept tossing his head and pawing fretfully at the ground with a front hoof. A bared .45 was in Gillenwater's hand but the barrel pointed earthward.

Ten feet from Gillenwater, Quinton halted the bay. "You're letting me through, Gillenwater," he cried, voice thick with rage and hurt. His thumb drew back the hammer of his .44. Gillenwater's eyes slitted ever so slightly as his ears caught the click. "You're letting me through or I'm putting a bullet in her back!"

The white stallion shied and Gillenwater reined it in with a savage jerk of the lines. The horse snorted a little in pain. The wide brim of Gillenwater's Stetson shaded his eyes so that the expression there was not visible. However, the line of his mouth under the black, drooping mustache was stiff and hard. A muscle kept twitching and writhing in his throat. The knuckles of his hand holding the .45 turned white. He said nothing.

Behind him, Quinton was aware that the other half of Anchor's riders had come to a halt. His glance stayed fixed on Gillenwater.

"You can kill me, Gillenwater," Quinton said, bearing down on the gun in Kate's back so that the added pressure ripped a hurt moan out of her, "but she'll die, too. You baited a nice trap but it isn't going to work the way you and her thought it would."

"No!" cried Kate Gillenwater, turning her head to throw a strained look at him. "No, Quinton. Not me. I knew nothing about it. He told me it was all right. He planned this after I left. I didn't—"

He gave another brutal shove on the gun that tore a shriek out of her. The words died strangling in her throat. Clay Gillenwater watched, his cheeks ashen with helpless fury. The gun in his hand rose an inch as if in the beginning of something. Then he changed his mind and the .45 sagged again.

The line of Quinton's jaw hardened. "I'm coming through, Gillenwater," he shouted. "Make a way for me. I'm coming through. You can shoot me down from the front and you can shoot me down from the back, but you can't stop me from putting a slug in her heart. So make a way for me. I'm coming through."

His rowels touched the bay and the horse responded. It moved up the slope at a walk. It passed Gillenwater's restless stallion and the white horse nickered nervously. The bay did not answer. It moved on.

Quinton could feel Gillenwater's glance on his back as he passed the man up. Quinton's flesh crawled. Another channel of sweat ran down the beard stubble on his cheeks.

Kate was tense in front of him. Her hands were clenched and her chin was tilted and the pulse throbbed visibly in her throat. Her eyes were glazed with the pain from the pressure of the gun in her back but she did not cry out any more. He could hear the taut, sibilant sound of her breathing.

The riders behind Gillenwater had formed a solid line but now, at a signal from him, they parted. Quinton sent the bay through the opening, still at a walk. His flesh kept flinching and recoiling in expectation of the impact of a bullet.

The bay moved on. The crest of the ridge drew nearer and still no shot had come from below. Kate's chin sagged abruptly and she began to cry. Her sobs were violent and racking, her shoulders heaved as if from hysteria, she grew slack and he had to hold her harder to keep her from sliding to the ground. As he listened to her, there was no pity in Quinton, no feeling other than a disillusioned rage.

The bay topped the summit of the ridge and as he was skylighted there the tantalizing thought came to Quinton that it had all been a brutal game and now the bullet would come. It was with an effort that he kept from raking the bay with the spurs. He started to turn his head to give a look back but then he caught himself and he kept his glance fixed straight ahead. The bay moved on and now they were below the crest.

Quinton lifted the bay into a lope, heading for some timber farther along the ridge. He was about to enter the trees when shouts came from the other side and then the roar of guns. On the instant, Quinton froze, heart in his throat. Then it dawned on him that this was not meant for him.

The shots had stilled Kate's crying. Her head was cocked to one side as she listened. The guns kept roaring. Someone screamed in pain and a horse squealed with hurt.

Keeping to the cover of the trees, Quinton urged the bay back up the slope. At the top he halted behind a pine and peered around this to witness the battle below.

The small ranchers had come down on Anchor from the opposite ridge. The whole scene below was a melee of wheeling, plunging horses and a deafening roar of gunfire. Quinton's eyes instantly picked out a slight figure on a paint horse. Stony Brice!

Brice rode doubled over as the paint streaked down the slope. He was heading straight for Clay Gillenwater who was trying to rally several of his men around a cluster of stones. The rest were fleeing.

Kate screamed a warning. Gillenwater could not hear her but something alerted him. He wheeled his white stallion and his gun blazed as he spotted Brice but Brice fired an instant before.

Gillenwater sagged in his saddle. The stallion lunged in fright as the grip on his reins slackened. The lurch unseated Gillenwater. He made a grab for the saddlehorn and missed. He fell with his arms and legs waving aimlessly as if he were already dead. He landed on his face and did not move.

Kate's face turned gray and suddenly she lowered it and put it in her hands. She shuddered once but no sounds of sorrow or remorse came from her. Quinton saw a horse with an empty saddle racing in terror up the ridge toward him and he loosened his hold on the woman so that she slid to the ground. She stood there, face still pressed into her palms, as Quinton took off in pursuit of the horse.

He roped the animal and led it back to where Kate Gillenwater was still standing. She had finally taken her hands away from in front of her face. There were creases at the corners of her mouth and a haunted luminosity glazed her eyes.

The gunfire on the other side of the ridge had slackened. Only scattered shots rang out. With the death of Clay Gillenwater, the remainder of his men had fled.

Quinton reined up and looked down at the woman. There was no feeling in him other than distaste and disgust. "Here's a horse," he said, his voice flat and toneless. "If you ride hard enough, you can make it back to Anchor."

She took the lines but she did not mount. She stood there looking up at him with pleading in her glance. "Are you coming with me?"

Rage blazed across his eyes. He came upright in his stirrups. "After what you did you've still got the gall to ask me that?" he shouted.

The paleness had reached her lips. They looked dry and wrinkled. A hint of moisture appeared at the corners of her eyes. "I tell you I had nothing to do with it, Quinton. He tricked me. He hated you for killing Dalhart and the others and for running out on Anchor. Maybe he even knew about you and me. He told me it would be all right for me to bring you back to Anchor. He said you could have Dalhart's job. I didn't know he was going to set a trap for you. I didn't know it any more than you did."

He started to wheel the bay but she reached up and caught the bridle, stopping the horse. "I'm all alone now, Quinton," she said, tears trickling down her cheeks. "I'm all alone and I need you. I need you very much. Don't ride out on me. Please?"

Seeing her cry moved nothing in him. He supposed it was all over, as cold and spent as the ashes of a long-dead fire. This, his first real love, was ended. He knew he would never have another.

Bitterness and disillusion swirled achingly in him. "You'll find someone," he said stiffly. "You won't have any trouble finding someone. Anchor's big enough and you're cheap enough."

She flinched as though he had struck her. "Please, Quinton," she cried. "Don't ride out on me. Not now. I need you to tell me what to do. Anchor's all mine now. You've got to tell me what to do."

"I can tell you all of it right now. Anchor's through. The war is over." It came to him at that moment that the shooting had ceased entirely. "Forget your big ideas. Get along with your neighbors. You'd better get along because if you don't Anchor will go under."

With a vicious jerk on the lines he ripped the bridle out of her grip and turned the bay. She cried out as if she had been hurt. He paid her no heed. He touched the bay with the spurs and the horse moved off through the trees.

Behind him, Kate shouted, "Anchor will never go under. Do you hear, Quinton?" The tears were gone from her voice, and the pleading. It was thick and hoarse with savage wrath. "Anchor is far from through. Instead of the end, this is just the beginning. Do you hear me? Anchor will never quit and it will never be through. Remember that, Quinton!"

He spurred the bay into a run, keeping to the trees. He tried dismissing her from his mind but her image persisted tormentingly in front of his eyes. He cursed and tried to think of what she should do next. His mind, however, would have none of this. It could think only of his hopeless, misplaced love.

He turned back toward the heights from which he had just come. Perhaps in the solitude of the mountains he could thrash it out. Right now he was beyond thinking anything out rationally. His mind was too full of the debris of his shattered dreams.

He rode along, immersed in the pain of dis-illusionment, and he was only vaguely aware he had emerged from the timber. The bay moved along at the base of an outcropping of stone which made a sharp bend inward. As Quinton rode around this, awareness returned to him abruptly and stunningly, causing him to rein in the bay so sharply that it reared high.

As the bay's front hoofs came down to earth again, a cold hand closed about Quinton's heart. There ahead of him, sitting relaxed in his saddle, gun trained unwaveringly and menacingly on Quinton's middle was Stony Brice.

Chapter 13

Brice's pale eyes mirrored nothing. The boyish features were inscrutable, displaying no more expression than the icy heights of the White Peaks. The big bore of his Remington .44-40, however, was more than eloquent.

Quinton's right hand rose shoulder high. There was a sinking feeling in his stomach as he thought, "Maybe at last he knows who I really am." There was no fear in Quinton, however. The aftermath of bitter delusion was still too strong for him to care about anything else.

Brice sent the paint ahead until it was alongside the bay. Brice plucked the .44 out of Quinton's holster. Then Brice reined his paint away and put up his Remington. The corners of Brice's mouth quirked in that chill, slight resemblance to the beginning of a smile.

"I didn't want you to get the wrong idea and go for your iron," Brice said, hefting Quinton's .44. "I mean you no harm, Quinton."

Quinton was too astonished to speak.

"You don't believe me?" said Brice, recognizing Quinton's doubt. "We know about Dalhart."

"How?" asked Quinton.

"Word about a thing like that gets around fast."

Suddenly Brice tossed the .44 and Quinton caught it. Brice folded his wrists over his saddlehorn. "I guess we had you tallied wrong right from the beginning, Quinton. We should have hired you on that day you came out to Bar H Bar. As it turned out, however, you helped us even more by going to work for Anchor."

Quinton looked down at the .44 in his right hand, his heart beating rapidly. He could hardly believe his eyes. Brice suspected nothing. He was sitting there in his kak relaxed and unsuspicious. Excitement pounded in Quinton's blood. This was his chance. This was the chance he had begun to doubt would ever come.

He was about to raise the gun and point it at Brice and have the whole thing finally over with when the sound of running horses came from behind him. Guiltily, he whipped around in the saddle and saw Wes Hawthorne and Red Armour riding up. Hawthorne stopped his horse alongside Brice's paint. Red Armour, however, reined in behind Quinton. Armour's eyes were narrowed and hostile.

Reluctantly, Quinton holstered his weapon. He told himself there would be another time. Now that peace had come to the White Peaks, he could take Stony Brice any time he wanted to.

Wes Hawthorne was breathing heavily with excitement and happiness. His eyes shone. "We've licked them, Stony," he cried.

"Gillenwater's dead. There's no one to lead them any more. We've won, Stony!"

This appeared to make no impression on Brice. His face remained as inscrutable as ever. "Let's not count our horses until the last one's in the corral, Wes."

Hawthorne looked puzzled. "What else can they do? Gillenwater's dead and so is Dalhart." His excited glance swung to Quinton. "We heard about you getting Dalhart and those others, Quinton. You sure helped us there."

Red Armour made a derisive sound behind Quinton. Hawthorne laughed and kneed his horse over beside Quinton's bay. Hawthorne raised a hand and clapped Quinton on the back. "Red still hasn't got over you getting the drop on him that time, Quinton, but don't mind him. He'll come around." Hawthorne's face clouded then, his exuberance gone. "I ran you off Bar H Bar once," he said humbly and contritely, "but now I know how wrong I was. I want you to know that you're welcome there, Quinton. You're welcome there as long as you want to stay. I'd be proud to have you working for me."

Quinton told himself that the reason he rode to Bar H Bar was that it kept him close to Stony Brice. The ordeal of the past few days had Quinton on the verge of exhaustion. He needed several days of rest. When he felt up to it, he would arrest Brice and then start on the long journey back to the Trinity.

But there was something else in his mind, something mocking and insidious which told him that there was another reason he was staying in the White Peaks. After refusing to acknowledge it, he finally had to admit the truth. Kate Gillenwater was still on his mind.

Despite the pain and disillusionment, he still loved her. This love was something that transcended hurt and deceit and guile. It had rooted itself too deeply in his heart for him to put it aside casually. He realized achingly that he could never put it aside. Good or bad, right or wrong, it was something he could not help. He had to go along with it until the day he died.

This knowledge left him grave and moody. He was leaning against a corral post the next day, smoking and thinking on this, when spur tinkle caused him to lift his head and he saw Stony Brice crossing the yard toward him. Brice's hat was perched on the back of his head and his rounded cheeks gave him the appearance of an innocent boy so that the twin, tied-down Remingtons looked incongruous on either side of his hips.

Brice stopped and got out the makin's and for a while gave all his attention to the building of a cigarette. When he had it lighted, he lifted his head and looked at Quinton. A while Brice smoked, pale eyes opaque through the tobacco smoke curling up in front of them.

Finally Brice said, "What made you leave Texas, Quinton?"

The old caution made Quinton suddenly tense inside. "Didn't I tell you a couple times? Just drifting."

"I know," said Brice, studying the end of his cigarette. "That's the reason I give for leaving Texas, too. But I had no choice." His glance lifted and speared Quinton's face. "Was it like that with you?"

"Maybe," said Quinton.

"I don't think so." Brice's tone was soft but flat.

Something tingled the back of Quinton's neck. "I don't know what you mean," he said carefully.

"You're as hard as anybody," said Brice, the skin on his cheeks drawn a little now. "You proved that the way you handled Dalhart and his compadres. You're a top hand with a gun, Quinton, but you're no hired gunman. Why have you stayed in the White Peaks?"

"Why have you?" Quinton countered. "Why have you worked for Hawthorne when Anchor would have paid you several times as much?"

Brice did not answer right away. The focus of his eyes shifted and for once a slight expression entered them. They looked grave and reflective, as if he were searching his soul for some truth that had eluded him.

"I'm a killer, Quinton," he said in his soft, gentle way. "I guess I'll be a killer as long as I live, which may not be much." The edges of his mouth quirked in what was as much of a smile as he ever achieved. "I haven't contributed much to the world, only hell-raising and killing. With the life I lead I can't expect anything but to die young. I figured that I might as well do one right thing before I get killed." He shrugged. "So I went to work for Bar H Bar instead of Anchor. After all, money won't mean anything to me after I'm in boothill. On the other hand, it makes me feel good inside to know that for once I was on the right side. It can't make up for the men I've killed. Nothing can ever make up for that. But since it's cut out for me to kill, I might as well do the killing for those who are in the right." His eyes shifted back to Quinton. They were agate hard and opaque again. "Can you understand a thing like that, Quinton?"

Quinton nodded. He felt strangely moved so that he could not speak. Brice's sincerity had touched Quinton and he did not like it. He could feel himself being drawn sympathetically toward this, slight, boyish-looking killer and this was the one thing Quinton wished to avoid. His job was to arrest Brice, not form an attachment for him.

"I've answered your question," Brice went on quietly, "but you haven't answered mine."

Quinton stirred irritably. He dropped his smoke

205

and ground it out under his heel with more force than was necessary. There was something he could not explain, to Brice or any one else.

"I thought I'd pick up some of the big money Anchor was paying," he said slowly, "but then I found I couldn't go along with what they were doing. So I quit."

"Is that all?" asked Brice.

Quinton turned a keen glance on Brice's face but there was nothing on it that could be read. "What else could there be?" he parried.

"Why didn't you leave the White Peaks when you quit Anchor? Why did you hang around the mountains? Why have you come here to Bar H Bar? You aren't happy here. I can see that. Yet you stay on. What's keeping you?"

You, Brice, Quinton said to himself, and Kate. She was the real reason he was staying on in the White Peaks. She was the reason he was postponing the arresting of Brice. He wanted to see her once more. No matter what she had done to him, he wanted to ask her to go away with him. When she agreed to that, he would arrest Brice and leave these mountains, not before.

"Maybe I'm tired of drifting," he said after a while. "I'd like to sink roots somewhere and stay the rest of my life. Why not in the White Peaks?"

Brice considered this a while. His cigarette had burned down to a butt, but he held it until it must have singed his fingers. He dropped it finally and stepped on it with a detached pensiveness. The round outlines of his features told nothing of what went on in him.

"If that's the way it is," Brice said quietly, "then I wish you luck. If not—"

He shrugged and turned away.

Luke Fowler rode in that noon. He nodded genially to Quinton and exchanged a few remarks about the weather. Fowler expressed no surprise at seeing Quinton at Bar H Bar nor did Fowler make any comment on the killing of Dalhart. Fowler went into the house with Wes Hawthorne and the two men conversed for about an hour.

There was a spring to Fowler's step when he emerged. He waved an arm in farewell to Quinton and Brice and rode away, straight in the saddle. West Hawthorne was beaming as he watched the white-haired rancher go.

"He's going to see Kate Gillenwater," Hawthorne said to Quinton and Brice. "He's going to talk her into ending this war. He's pretty sure he can do it, now that Gillenwater and Dalhart are dead." Hawthorne sighed and a plaintive look came into his eyes. "It'll be good to have peace in the White Peaks again," he said wistfully.

Brice kicked at a pebble on the ground. His head was bowed. "I hope you and Fowler are right," he murmured.

Surprise widened Hawthorne's eyes. "What else can she do? She has no choice." Then Hawthorne smiled. "You take things too seriously, Stony. Relax. Everything will work out. Luke will bring the good word tomorrow. You just watch and see."

"I hope you're right," Brice said again, still staring at the ground.

Quinton made no comment. In the privacy of his mind he was agreeing with Stony Brice.

When Luke Fowler returned the next morning, the iron was gone from his spine. He rode slouched in the saddle, a tired old man who looked like he had finally surrendered to the futility of life. His bleak eyes held a cynicism that had never been there before.

He reined in his buckskin and after he had dismounted, he leaned his head against the saddle in a gesture of utter weariness. Before anyone could reach him, however, he recovered. His shoulders squared and his chin lifted and when he turned around he was cold, grim old man with a determined glint in his clear, direct glance.

Wes Hawthorne, features tight with anxiety, was staring fixedly at Fowler. Hawthorne's mouth opened once as if he were going to speak, then either words failed him or he changed his mind for his lips closed without uttering a sound.

Stony Brice watched with that faint quirk at the corners of his mouth. However, there was no amusement in this slight expression. It was just the reflection of an old skepticism.

Bitterness roiled Quinton as he waited for Fowler to speak. Quinton could sense what was coming and, although it was disappointing, it was not a surprise. He realized with a measure of disgust and loathing that it could have been no other way.

Luke Fowler did not waste words. "She'll have none of it," he said grimly.

Wes Hawthorne frowned. He shook his head as if he could not comprehend. "But she has no choice," he exclaimed. "Gillenwater and Dalhart and most of the gunslingers are dead. Marberry is the only gunman left. We've licked Anchor at every turn. What makes her think she can win when Anchor couldn't with Gillenwater, Dalhart and the others?"

Fowler sighed. His sad eyes had a faraway look in them as though he were pondering wistfully on what might have been. "She says she has already sent to Texas for more gunmen. She says the war hasn't started yet. She says we're either going to leave the White Peaks or be buried here." A melancholy gravity lay in the hollowing of his cheeks. "I think she means every word of it."

Hawthorne swore. Wrath had begun to tint his features. His mouth quivered with anger. "We'll fight her then," he declared, the line of his jaw hard and adamant. "No one's running me out of the White Peaks, least of all a woman. I'll die before I give up Bar H Bar."

Luke Fowler said nothing. His eyes were bleak and old with a sorry, distasteful wisdom. He looked like he had finally, abruptly lost his faith in man and was left with no replacement to sustain him.

Stony Brice rolled a cigarette with steady fingers. That faint, mirthless shadow of a smile still lingered at the edges of his mouth. He struck a match, lighted his cigarette and blew out a great cloud of smoke. His eyes lost their opaqueness long enough to display a brief glint of a savage and lustful cruelty.

"We'll let her call the game," he said in his quiet, toneless way. "Then we'll make her wish she had never come to the White Peaks . . ."

That night Anchor rode again. They struck at Keyhole which lay next to Bar H Bar. The faint sound of shooting floated over the hills in the chill night air. The keen ears of the dog picked up the almost imperceptible noise and he set up a loud insistent barking which wakened Hawthorne, Brice and Quinton.

As soon as they made out the sound of shooting, the three saddled their horses and rode at a swift gallop for Keyhole. While still some distance away they saw the crimson, flickering reflection of a fire against the black immensity of the sky.

The sound of shooting had ceased now. The night was full of a portentous silence broken only by the drumming of the horses' hoofs.

They found all of Keyhole's buildings ablaze. One wall of the barn caved in as they rode up. Red Armour and the one hand he employed were both dead.

Wes Hawthorne cursed steadily in impotent, furious anger. He raised a fist once and brandished it in the direction of Anchor, cursing all the while. Now and then his voice broke, in imitation of a sob of helpless grief.

In the carmine light of the fire, Stony Brice's expressionless features looked almost cherubic but that was before one took a glance at his eyes. They were alive and glittering.

"Tomorrow night will be our night," was all he said.

At noon the next day Luke Fowler showed up at Bar H Bar accompanied by his five riders. All of them were heavily armed. Fowler's face looked wan and drawn, mirroring the turmoil that stormed in him.

"It's either us or Anchor," he announced grimly. "We've got to end it once and for all. Tonight Anchor goes. No matter what the cost, Anchor has to go. The rattler's nest will have to be cleaned out. I've stayed out of the fighting so far but I can't stay out any more."

Word was sent out to the other small ranchers and at evening they began drifting in to Bar H Bar, every man who could ride a horse and shoot a gun. They were a hard, silent group. Their attitude revealed that they were all ready to die if that was the one means of ending this conflict in the White Peaks.

Quinton saddled his bay and led him from the corral. Luke Fowler walked over. He had assumed command this day with no protests or visible resentment from Brice. Fowler's long familiarity with Anchor indicated that he was the man to lead the others.

"Are you riding with us, Quinton?" asked Fowler.

Quinton nodded. He said nothing.

In the gathering shadows, Fowler's face appeared to have softened. Quinton could feel the man's glance picking at his face.

"You don't have to," Fowler said softly, although they were out of earshot of the others.

Quinton didn't say anything to this either. He was staring at the ground without seeing it. The image of a bronze-haired woman had come in front of his eyes, momentarily obliterating everything else.

Fowler cleared his throat. He seemed rather uncomfortable. "I know how it must be with you," he went on in that quiet, intimate tone. "No one will question your courage if you stay behind.

212

You've proved it already. It—it won't be very nice, Quinton." He spoke in a pained, troubled way.

Quinton lifted his head. His mouth was hard. His bleak glance passed over the group of men readying their horses. Quinton barely saw them.

"I want to be there to see how it comes out," he said stiffly.

"I—I tried to tell you once what she was like."

A fit of disgusted anger swept through Quinton. He told himself he had no one to get angry with but himself. "I know what she's like," he said, growling a little. "I've known it all the time."

In the gloom he could feel Fowler's glance searching his face. "Yet you couldn't help yourself. Is that how it is, Quinton?" Fowler's voice was soft with compassion.

Quinton said nothing. He stared off without seeing anything.

Fowler sighed. It was something soft and sad, like the dying of a dream. "She's no better than her husband was. She might even have egged him on. He certainly changed after he married her. No one knows much about her except that she always was an opportunist. I'm quite sure she never loved Clay. She married him because of Anchor. Now she has Anchor and she means to have all of the White Peaks if she can. That's why we've got to stop her, Quinton. She's rotten all the way through."

Hearing these words put a pang in Quinton's heart because he knew they were true. Quinton could not resent them. They were cold, naked facts and there was no point in trying to deny them.

"Well, what are we waiting for?" he asked harshly. "Isn't it time we started?"

Fowler kept his glance on Quinton a moment longer. The old man's eyes were sad and contemplative. He seemed about to say something, then changed his mind. He wheeled abruptly and went over to his buckskin. As he swung into the saddle, the others followed suit. Fowler raised his right arm in a signal and then started the buckskin off at a brisk trot.

Chapter 14

A feeling of doom settled over Quinton as the cavalcade left Bar H Bar. At first, he attributed this uneasiness to what obviously lay ahead. There would be violence, and undoubtedly, dying. Perhaps he was included among those whose turn it was to die tonight. But it was not this that was weighing on his mind. He had been face to face with death so often as to have acquired an almost contemptuous familiarity with it.

It was Kate Gillenwater first and foremost in his thoughts. He could not shake her image from his brain. The closer they drew to Anchor the sharper and more poignant the recollection of her became.

What made it so irritating and tantalizing was the knowledge that though they loved each other they were worlds apart in nature. She had that twisted quirk in her mind, the overpowering urge of ambition and greed that made her mean and ruthless, though right now he could think only of how fervent and tender she had been in his arms. It was this remembrance that put the old ache back in his throat. It was this memory that filled him with a sudden rush of hungry longing. Then reason prevailed and he put this feeling from his mind. He thought of the Coreys and Red Armour and Bucky Dean, and even Gillenwater and Dalhart and all the others dead because of her covetousness. The emotion he was experiencing now closely approximated hate.

He tried consoling himself with the thought that tonight the thing might finally be ended. If Anchor's power was broken, there would be nothing to keep him in the White Peaks any longer. Tomorrow, if he was not dead, he would finally arrest Stony Brice and start on the long way back to the Trinity. He resolved he would not put it off beyond tomorrow. He had hesitated much too long. Thinking thus afforded him some consolation although not as much as he would have liked.

They reached Anchor at midnight. The men had been well briefed in advance and they went about their assignments without delay or confusion. Half of them dismounted while still some distance from the buildings and proceeded the rest of the way on foot, stealthily. They worked their way in until they had the bunkshack surrounded. Anchor had two men on guard but Quinton knew where these were stationed and he had so informed Fowler. The two guards were overwhelmed without an outcry from them.

Fowler had asked Quinton to stay beside him. Brice was in charge of the group that had gone in on foot. Fowler and Quinton sat on their

216

horses on a little rise just beyond the buildings of Anchor.

Fowler drew his .44 Starr and held it in his hands a while. His shot was to be the signal but he seemed to hesitate. His head was bowed a little as though he were dwelling on some recollections that had to do with the old days when he had helped build this ranch and had ramrodded it for Colonel Gillenwater. He appeared very much taken up with his thoughts so that the Starr remained unfired in his hand.

Finally Fowler's hand lifted. Quinton heard the old man as he sucked in a great ragged breath. The barrel of the Starr tipped skyward and stayed like that a few moments in a final burst of reluctance and indecision. Then an old thumb cocked the hammer. That ragged inhalation of breath sounded again. The Starr roared.

The shot made a flat, whip-like crack. Flame lanced out of the bore of the Starr and even before the echoes began having their way with the sound, a crash of gunfire came from ahead.

Fowler's head dipped. His shoulder sagged. In the darkness, angling through the vicious roaring of the guns, there came to Quinton another sound. It was the sound of an old man crying.

Guns were barking from within the bunkshack now. A gun also started working from the big house and the thought came instantly to Quinton. Kate! But that was all the time he gave to it. A slug whined past his head, a wild shot since he and Fowler could not be seen. Quinton grabbed the bridle of Fowler's buckskin and led him into the shelter of some trees. Fowler sat slumped in his saddle, unaware that his horse was moving. He was still crying, softly.

The rest of the small ranchers rode in now, their guns adding to the din. The red glow of a fire began, flickering at first, then flaring with a vile, carmine brightness. There were yells and scattered screams. From where he was watching, Quinton could see the shadowy figures of men racing from the bunkshack. They were going to get out before the firelight expanded and made them sharply etched targets.

The gun in the big house became silent and Quinton's heart shriveled in him. No, his mind cried out, no. A sense of dread, of a great and tardy remorse closed about him. He could feel the urge rising in him to ride in there and find out what had happened to her. His teeth clenched and his nails bit into the palms of his balled hands.

Quinton told himself she was probably reloading her gun but the time passed and he knew sinkingly that it would not take long to refill the magazine of a Winchester. The roaring of the guns continued undiminished but Quinton was aware only of the silence in the big house.

Fowler lifted his head and wiped his eyes. He no longer wept.

The fire was expanding, the bunkshack was aflame. In the spreading range of the firelight, Quinton saw several riders break away. One of them went tumbling out of the saddle just as his horse was about to pass into the darkness. Though he strained his eyes, Quinton had been unable to discern the identity of the horsemen. He knew only that they were Anchor. He had been unable to tell if Kate Gillenwater had been one of them.

The gun in the big house had not yet resumed firing.

Then it was over. Gunfire ceased and now there was only the crackling of the flames and the shouts of men. Someone threw a flaming brand on the roof of the big stone house and the dried shingles quickly caught fire.

In this light, Fowler and Quinton came riding up. A sickening dread pawed among Quinton's entrails. His eyes strained anxiously to look and were at the same time afraid of what they might see. He told himself he should not feel this way. If she was dead, it was no more than she deserved. It had been her decision alone that had prolonged the conflict and brought it to this.

Someone had brought Stony Brice his paint horse and he rode over to Fowler and Quinton, who had reined in and were watching the flames eating away at the roof of the big house. Brice's face was as expressionless as ever although his eyes glittered brightly.

"Half a dozen of them got away," Brice announced. "I'm going after them."

Quinton felt his heart skip a beat. On the moment his throat filled so that he doubted he could get any words out, but it cleared and he heard himself saying, "What about Mrs. Gillenwater?" His voice sounded harsh.

Brice's glance shifted and studied Quinton an instant. There was something cautious and speculative in it. Then Brice said, "She's one of those who got away . . ."

They trailed the fleeing Anchor riders up toward the heights of the White Teaks. The pace slowed down as the morning progressed, for the horses of both pursuers and pursued were badly tired. At first, the Anchor men had stayed in one group. Now that they were up in the isolated reaches of the White Peaks they scattered out. Their pursuers also broke up.

Two of the Anchor riders were cornered in a box canyon. They put up a fight at first but one of them was quickly wounded and his partner abruptly lost his taste for resistance and surrendered.

Another Anchor hand who had decided to try it alone was spotted as he was riding along a ledge. Rifle fire opened up from below. A slug doubled him up in the saddle and then his horse reared and threw him. He hit the rim of the ledge and seemed to teeter tantalizingly there. His fingers clawed frenziedly as he started to roll the wrong way but there was nothing for them to grab. He screamed as he went over the rim and he kept on screaming until, halfway down, his head smashed against a boulder. He rolled the remainder of the way with his arms and legs waving grotesquely.

Quinton had become separated from the others. He followed the tracks of a lone horse but the sign petered out on the bank of a creek. He had to scout both banks of the stream, up and down, for an hour before he picked the tracks up again. Only now there were the tracks of two horses, one of them trailing the other.

A sinking sensation struck the pit of Quinton's stomach. He tried reassuring himself with the thought that this might not be Kate but there was no way he could be positive. Even if this wasn't her, she was somewhere else and wherever she was, she was being trailed. Perhaps she had already been run down. Perhaps she was already dead.

Quinton swore savagely and forcibly put this line of thinking from his mind. He felt all mixed up and sick inside. He did not rightly know what he was doing here. He knew only that he wanted to find her. Beyond that he could not think.

The bay was tired but Quinton spurred it on into a faster pace. Now and then its step faltered but Quinton knew no pity, no remorse. He had never in his life driven any horse so relentlessly and mercilessly as he was driving the bay right now.

He crossed a small plateau covered with trees and then the tracks led up a slope. His heart was pounding anxiously as he reached high ground. He reined in the bay momentarily, hoping to catch sight of something, but the country was too mottled with trees and brush for Quinton to spot anything. He cursed and spurred the unwilling bay on.

The tracks wound down the shoulder of a ridge. The trees began to thin out, large slabs of rock littered the land. It was becoming possible to see a long way and a remnant of hope surged in Quinton. The bay stumbled and almost went down. Quinton pulled it up with a hard jerk of the lines and spurred it on.

The tracks led around an outcropping of rock and as Quinton made this turn he saw the palomino. The palomino's saddle was empty. The palomino was lame.

Quinton came up sharply in his stirrups, harried eyes sweeping the land beyond and above him. Kate! It was a silent, twisted cry in his mind. Kate! A wave of anguish wrenched his heart.

He saw the other horse then, standing with hanging head among some brush, a hundred feet ahead. This horse was a paint. Brice! Thought of this name folded a clammy hand about Quinton's heart. A sense of urgency rose in him almost to the point of panic.

His first jab of the spurs failed to budge the exhausted bay. He jabbed again, with brutal, heedless force, and the bay squealed and moved on.

Kate!

The bay was blowing hard, its breath a whistling shriek in its throat. Its lathered flanks heaved and shuddered convulsively, its legs trembled with each step it took. It reached the paint which also was well done in. The paint did not so much as twitch an ear in acknowledgment of the presence of another of its kind. The paint stood on straddled legs, hanging muzzle almost touching the earth, the heaving of its flanks the only movement it generated.

Kate!

Quinton's apprehensive glance picked up the boot tracks going up the slope. He raked the bay with the spurs. The horse responded for several steps, then abruptly went down on its front knees. It tried valiantly to rise, getting one hoof on the ground, but when it tried to come the rest of the way it lacked the strength. It went down on both knees again and swayed to the side as if it were going to topple over. His heart beating like the throbbing of an urgent drum, Quinton pulled his Winchester from its saddle scabbard and stepped to the ground.

The swift, anxious probing of his eyes spied something on the slope above. Squinting his eyes while his heart raced fearfully, he waited a moment and caught it again. A red plaid jacket and then the flaming of bronze hair in the sun.

"Kate!"

He cried it aloud this time. It seemed to tear the bottom out of his heart and it was now that he finally, irrevocably realized how much he loved her. It was her for him, now and always, good or bad, through ruin and death.

She was scrambling up the slope toward the shelter of some stones farther on but she paused as though she had heard him. Her head turned and just as she glimpsed him down below, brandishing his rifle, the shot rang out.

"Kate!" The tortured, stricken shout clawed at the walls of Quinton's throat. "Kate!"

She appeared to shudder and sag. She sank to her knees but she caught herself there. She had a carbine in her hands and now she started to bring the gun up to her shoulder. Another shot cracked the indifferent stillness of the mountains. The carbine dropped unfired from her hands and she pitched over on her back.

"Kate!"

It was all grief now, overflowing his heart, welling up out of his throat. The tears were hot on the planes of his cheeks, tears of anguish and rage. Cursing, he brushed them away and looked farther down the slope and there he saw Brice.

Quinton's shouts had brought Brice around, rifle held ready at his hip. He was crouched over, head ducked down, watching Quinton warily out of upraised eyes, boyish face as indifferent as though he had just shot a tin can off a fence post.

Quinton sucked in a big breath that felt as though it would burst his lungs. Through all the torment came the knowledge that the long manhunt was finally over. There was nothing to keep him in the White Peaks any more. The thing that had kept him here now lay with the stillness of death on the slope above. At long last he could do what he had come all the way from Trinity to do. But he did not want it just exactly that way.

"Bryan!" he shouted, voice thick with anguish and hate, and saw Brice jerk as though he had been struck a tremendous blow. "Steve Bryan!" he cried again, and saw the mask of indifference drop from Brice's features. Shock and surprise set Brice's mouth agape. His slight body came up straight. He stood there all tense and stunned, one corner of his mouth twitching spasmodically.

"I've come all the way from the Trinity for you," Quinton went on, face flushed with fury, eyes luminous with a savage purpose. The cords bulged and writhed in his neck. "I am a deputy sheriff and you know what I want you for. It is my duty to ask you to surrender and return with me to the Trinity to stand trial. If you surrender I promise you that is what I'll do. But I don't want you to surrender!"

He drew in another breath that made a sound

like a racking sob. Grief was a suffocating wad in his chest, it hurt him to breathe, it hurt him not to. His hands were trembling from the force of the wrath and bereavement in him.

"This is for her," he shouted, brandishing his rifle at a spot up the slope. "This is between me and you for her. I want you to know that, Brice. I want you to know that because I am going to kill you if you don't surrender."

Brice fired. The slug took Quinton in the chest and slammed him back. On the instant, all feeling passed from his fingers and the Winchester fell from his grip. He felt his spurs tangle with something and then he was sitting down hard. He knew he had been hit and he wondered that he felt no pain, only a strange, dull numbness in his breast.

Brice fired again, this time also from the hip, but Quinton was already going down and the shot missed. Brice leveled another cartridge home and whipped the rifle to his shoulder for a better aim.

Down on the ground, Quinton drew his .44. The first twinge of pain came from his chest. He could feel the numbness fading, he felt warm and moist there as though blood were starting to run, but the pain was only a shadow of reality.

He snapped off a shot with the .44. Brice fired also. Quinton heard the banshee shriek of the slug past his ear. Then he saw Brice shudder and sag. Quinton threw another shot that went wild for at the same instant a wave of blackness passed before his eyes and the whole world reeled and heaved about him.

He came to lying on his side. He had no idea how much time had elapsed, whether a second or an eternity. He knew pain now. His whole breast was aflame with it, agonizing shoots of it reached down to his toes and seared its way up to his brain. His eyes ached with it as he searched the slope above him for Brice.

He saw Brice lying face down on the earth but as Quinton watched Brice pushed himself up on one elbow. He had lost his rifle but he pulled one of his Remingtons. He shook his head as he peered down the slope as though trying to clear something from in front of his eyes. Then he spotted Quinton. Sun glinted off metal as Brice lifted the big .44-40.

Quinton's gaze had steadied and he took careful aim. When he fired, the Remington fell silent from Brice's hand. His head dropped and for a while he hung suspended there, supporting himself on one elbow. Then the strength left him and he dropped. He gave a convulsive twist that brought him arching up in the air and when he came down he rolled down the slope a little way. He was making feeble attempts to draw his other Remington.

Quinton started crawling up the slope, dragging himself along on elbows and knees. Kate, the cry wailed in him, Kate. Something was screaming in him to hurry and even all the hurry in the world would not be enough.

He came to Brice. The man was not yet dead. His eyes were glazed, his gaping, gasping mouth had a trickle of blood coming out of one corner, but instinct had closed the fingers about the butt of his second Remington and had drawn it, although he could no longer see where to shoot.

Quinton paused long enough to thrust the bore of his .44 against Brice's temple. This slug stilled Stony Brice forever.

Quinton kept on doggedly up the slope. There were times when his mind began spinning down into the black maw of death and it was then that the urgency screamed more frantically than ever in his brain. But he would not yield to it. Kate, the cry mourned in him, Kate. He gasped and sobbed and crawled on, leaving a trail marked by a trickle of blood.

For him, an eternity passed and another one began, and then he reached her. The tears were dry on his cheeks as he pushed himself up on both elbows to get a look at her.

She lay as she had fallen, on her back, her bronze hair fanned out in a frame for her face. She had died easily, with her eyes closed and features uncontorted. The mouth looked grave and even a little sad.

A sob racked Quinton and then no more. The thought came to him that he had always known it would end like this. That was the meaning of those inklings of doom that had disturbed him ever since the first time he had seen her.

There were no more tears in him, even the grief seemed to be fading. He bent his head and kissed her unfeeling lips. A gulfing wave of darkness bore down on him. In its approach he could glimpse the inevitableness of death. Strength deserted him and he sagged beside her. There seemed to be something sweet and comforting in the knowledge that he would die beside her.

The last thing he saw was the shimmering of the sun in a mass of bronze hair.

About the Author

H(enry) A(ndrew) DeRosso was born on July 15, 1917, in Carey, Wisconsin. This area, in the northeast corner of the state near the Michigan border, is rich in its own pioneer history. Carey and its neighboring community of Hurley in which DeRosso made his home for many years were once rough-and-tumble iron-ore mining towns not unlike the gold, silver, and copper camps of the Far West frontier. This rural milieu, with its harsh winters and its proximity to the vast North Woods, may explain DeRosso's early interest in adventure and Western fiction and his lifelong fascination with the southwestern desert country, a wilderness and a climate exactly opposite of the one in which he lived. He began producing Western short stories while a high-school student, making his first professional sale to Street & Smith's *Western Story Magazine* in 1941. Health problems kept him out of military service during World War II, and thus he was able to continue writing on a daily basis and to begin piling up sales to *Western Story* and other pulps during this period, supplementing his income with farm work and as a mail carrier. By the end of the war he had established himself to the point where he was able to devote his full time to writing. Nearly all of his tales are set in the stark, desolate wastes of the Southwest. In the decades between 1940 and 1960 he published approximately two hundred Western short stories and short novels in various pulp magazines that became known for their dark and compelling visions of the night side of life and their austere realism. He was also the author of six Western novels, perhaps the most notable of which are *.44* (1953) and *End of the Gun* (1955). He died on October 14, 1960. Most recently his short stories are being collected by Bill Pronzini and published as Five Star Westerns, including *Under the Burning Sun* (1997) and *Riders of the Shadowlands* (1999).

Center Point Large Print
600 Brooks Road / PO Box 1
Thorndike, ME 04986-0001 USA

(207) 568-3717

US & Canada:
1 800 929-9108
www.centerpointlargeprint.com